Never Look Back

Coming Home:

Book two

Amy Stephens

Katie,

Thanks so much for your support.

Amy Stephens

Never Look Back, second edition

Copyright © 2014, 2016 by Amy Stephens

All rights reserved.

This is a work of fiction. Names, characters, businesses, places, events, and incidents are either the products of the author's imagination or used in a fictitious manner. Any resemblance to actual persons, living or dead, or actual events is purely coincidental.

This book or any portion thereof may not be reproduced or used in any manner whatsoever without the express written permission of Amy Stephens, except for the use of brief quotations embodied in critical articles and reviews.

Cover design by Amy Stephens

Images courtesy of Shutterstock / Nikita Starichenko

Prologue

Brian

One hundred fifty-one.

One hundred fifty-two.

One hundred fifty-three.

That's the number of cars that have passed since I started counting them almost two hours ago.

One hundred fifty-four.

One hundred fifty-five.

Suddenly, out of the corner of my eye, I spot a white, mid-size sedan headed east towards the interstate. I lean up from my crouched position in the front seat to get a better view, but it's no use. Red taillights—it's all I'm able to see.

I continue to stare at the bright red glare until the lights are so faint they eventually disappear altogether. So many white cars have passed, I'm not surprised I can't distinguish one from the other. This one particular car, though, makes me think of her.

Jennifer. Could it be? Could it really be her?

One hundred fifty-two...Fifty-three.

Shit! I've lost count. That damn white car distracted me, and I lost the number I was on. It's just as well. Who really gives a fuck how many cars I've counted anyway?

Without wasting anymore time, I crank my car. I need to know if it's her. The tires squeal as I pull out from the parking lot and into oncoming traffic. I hardly even see the pick-up truck that I narrowly miss. His blaring horn pulls me from the stupor I'm in. Then, it pisses me off even more when the driver flips the lights on high-beam. I stick my arm up and make a hand gesture, but I know it isn't seen. Not with it being dark and those damn bright lights shining. Right now, the only thing I'm concerned with is catching up to that white car.

I have a flashback from earlier and I'd give anything to take it all back. What the hell was I thinking throwing that damn bottle? For crying out loud, what kind of husband does that kind of thing? Mad or not, I shouldn't have done it.

Yet again, I was a complete moron.

She'd finally mustered the courage to tell me to leave. No, she demanded I get out right then. I guess I should consider myself lucky the neighbors didn't call the cops. They would've hauled me in seeing the mess I made in our apartment. Not to mention, the blood dripping from her cheek. And all because I lost my temper.

Why? Why do I always have to take things to the extreme? Why can't I just be man enough and own up to things?

When the wine bottle made contact with the sink, shards flew everywhere. I knew the moment it left my hand the damage it could do. But no, I was so caught up on blaming someone else, and I wasn't thinking with a clear hear. She kept covering up her stomach while her eyes pleaded with me. She was scared out of her wits. Then, she did a complete turnaround, and the look she gave me—hell, it had even scared me.

I know I'm a stupid asshole, but sometimes I just can't help myself. I get…I get so carried away that I lose control. Just like with my father. I have to believe it's not too late for me and Jennifer. *God, please tell me it's not too late. She's pregnant with our baby, and I…I just don't know what I'd do if I missed my baby being born.* There's got to be one more chance for me to prove to her. I promise I won't screw up again.

The light ahead turns yellow, and I see the white car come into my view. Maybe I can get close enough to see if it's her or not. I fidget in the seat and impatiently tap my fingers on the steering wheel. As soon as it changes green, I'm able to weave through a couple cars getting even closer. But then, then…I realize I'm nothing but an idiot—the car's not even white. It's a light gray color and nowhere near the same body style as hers.

I let off the gas and shake my head in frustration. I should've known it wasn't her anyway. Why would she be out this way in the first place?

The clock on the dash reads almost midnight. I make a U-turn at the next intersection and head back towards town. I drive pass several fast food places in addition to a few other retail establishments, including the hotel where Jennifer works. There's no reason to even pull through since it's her night off. If I hadn't lost my cool, I could be cuddled on the sofa with her right now instead of driving around in the middle of the night. Better yet, we could be making love to each other. *Damn it Brian! Now is not the time to be thinking about that.*

With no place to go, I weigh my options—I can continue driving around wasting gas or I can take my chances and go back to our apartment. Just maybe it's been a reasonable amount of time, and she's settled down enough to where we can at least talk. I decide on the latter. Hell, what do I have to lose?

I turn into the entrance of the apartment complex and follow the road all the way to the back where our unit is. As I round the corner, I find myself actually holding my breath. *Please don't let Rebecca's car be there.* To my surprise, though, her best friend's car isn't there and neither is Jennifer's. I immediately panic, fearing something serious may have happened. What if the cut on Jennifer's cheek was more than just a nick and she couldn't stop the bleeding? If she went to the hospital will the staff question her about how it happened? What kind of story would she tell them? Would she make up something to protect me or are the cops at the hospital making a report at this very moment?

I pull into my spot, place the car in park and glance around before shutting off the engine. Slowly, I climb out of the car while looking around. For a Saturday night, everything is eerily quiet. Sure, it's midnight, but something feels off.

I walk down the breezeway and stop just outside the front door. I lean forward and place my ear against it. Nothing. Not one single sound. I walk to the corner of the building, and, even though the blinds are closed, I can tell the living room lights are on. I walk back around, but I'm scared to touch the doorknob, fearful of what I might find on the other side. I pace the hallway a few moments, then figure what the heck. I insert my key into the lock but realize as soon as I turn it, the door isn't even locked.

I take a deep breath and push it open. The smell of the lasagna she'd had cooking lingers in the air. Although I haven't had anything to eat, there's no way I could stomach anything now, not with everything that's happened.

I notice a soft hum and soon figure out it's coming from the refrigerator. Other than that, the apartment is eerily silent. I step towards the kitchen. Bits of glass cover the countertop and is scattered across the floor. The pale yellow liquid from the bottle I threw has dried, leaving behind a sticky mess. I walk over to the sink to get a better look at things and hear pieces of glass crunch underneath my shoes. I stop when I notice the dried blood on the floor over in the corner next to the trash can. I follow a trail that leads from the kitchen to the hallway. I break out in a cold sweat as an image flashes through my mind--Jennifer crouched in the corner, curled up tightly so she could to protect our baby. She'd wanted to shield her face but her stomach and the baby was more important. I remember her hands coated in blood.

The room begins to spin. I can still hear her shouting.

"Get the hell away from me, Brian!"

I reach up to cover my ears. I just want the voices to stop.

"I said don't come near me, Brian!"

I stumble backwards. I bend over and place my hands on top of my knees, squeezing my eyes tightly shut. It's worse than I thought.

When I feel I've gotten ahold of myself, I make my way to the bathroom. The lights appear to be brighter than normal, making the pink rim left in the sink easier to see. *Oh my God!* A stained washcloth is crumpled in the bottom of the trashcan. I lean over to pull it out but it's…it's too…it's more than I can deal with. The beige colored washcloth is now a deep reddish-brown and ruined beyond use.

I immediately turn on the hot water in the sink and use my fingers to scrub away the remaining traces. I can't let anyone see this. The water is so hot and it scalds my hands, but I can't let this be discovered. I just can't. If the cops show up …how do I…how do I explain all this?

I pull a clean hand towel out of the drawer to dry my hands then cover my face with it. I'm sweating profusely. Of all the situations I've been in before nothing can compare to this. I stare at my reflection in the mirror and notice the countertop. Something's not right…something is missing. I snatch open the top drawer, and sure enough, things that should normally be here aren't. Jennifer's toothbrush, deodorant, hairdryer, and shampoo—they're all gone. The only things left are those that belong to me.

I try to remain calm as I walk to the bedroom. Sure enough, the closet reveals the same.

What the hell?

Where is everything? I pull out a few dresser drawers, but it's worse than I'd first thought. If she's gone to stay at Rebecca's, then why is there hardly anything left? Several hangers are scattered on the floor, and it appears as though Jennifer was in a hurry, snatching as much as possible.

Shit! Shit!

This is more than just an overnight stay. This looks like she's…gone.

I sit down on the side of the bed. I can't believe this is happening. I look around the room in shock of everything. My gaze stops on the nightstand. The bracelet I'd given her for

Christmas is sitting there. Jennifer was so happy when she'd opened up the box. I thought I'd done pretty well by surprising her with it, even if Rebecca did help me buy it. I chuckle under my breath. I still owe that bitch one last payment, but after the stunt she pulled earlier—the one where she turned my tray over on me--I seriously doubt she'll get it from me now. Screw her. It's all her fucking fault. Had she not run her god-damned mouth, I wouldn't be sitting her all alone.

I pick up the bracelet and rub my fingers over the stones. This was the nicest gift I'd ever given anyone. I'll find Jennifer and we'll work this out. We will patch this up again—we just have to. I will put this bracelet back on her arm and we will be happy together. I will prove to her Rebecca isn't the friend she thinks she is or needs, for that matter. She's got me and that's good enough. Rebecca's nothing but trouble—for her, for me, for us.

Devastated, I turn off the bedroom light and go back into the kitchen again. It's an absolute, horrific mess.

I grab the broom but soon realize it's going to take more than just sweeping to clean this up. I find a bottle of cleaner then fill the sink with hot water. I set to work scrubbing everything. I wipe down the countertops and walls, careful not to miss a spot. It's more work than I've ever had to do, but I'm determined to make the apartment spotless. I even mop the floors twice just to make sure I don't miss anything.

When I feel that the kitchen is clean enough, I move on to the living room and hallway. I know I should probably vacuum the floors first, but I worry that the noise from the vacuum cleaner will wake the neighbors. I do the best I can to pick up the glass pieces but the rest will have to wait 'til morning.

Rather than get on my hands and knees, I squat awkwardly and scrub the stains with a sponge. It's harder than I thought and doesn't take long before my legs begin to get stiff. I stand up to stretch then pat the pockets of my jeans and realize I've not had my cell phone on me this entire time. I curse myself for not checking earlier. What if Jennifer had tried to call?

Figuring I must've left it in the car, I go outside to search for it. I switch on the overhead light and finally find it on the floor of the passenger side.

I immediately check for any missed calls but a wave of disappointment consumes me.

Nothing.

No calls. No texts.

I consider calling her but stop at the last minute before pressing the send button. For once I'm glad her parents don't live here anymore. I could be dealing with her old man right about now. Fathers don't like guys who hurt their little girls.

Frustrated, I slowly walk back inside. I just knew she'd reach out to me. I don't even bother to lock the door behind me. I sit down on the sofa, exhausted from the night's events. It's no wonder women are always so tired when they've cleaned house all day. I look around the apartment and all I can think about is Jennifer. Where is she? Is she okay?

So, this is what it feels like when someone walks out on you.

Part One

Chapter 1

Jennifer

One month later

THERE'S NOTHING MORE RELAXING THAN sitting on the front porch, enjoying a cup of coffee and taking in a beautiful sunrise. I feel the fluttering sensation from the baby moving around inside my belly, and I place my hand over the spot. There's still a couple months left before I get to meet her, but I can't hardly wait. Although I'm nervous and excited, the time isn't passing quickly enough.

My mind drifts back to the past few weeks—it's been such an emotional rollercoaster ride with Brian. Oh, Brian, what did you do to me?

It's taken lots of courage on my part just to be where I am right now. Honestly, I never knew I had it in me. I'd just taken all that I could. I'd had enough.

That night was the final straw.

No one can ever say I don't believe in second chances, or even a third, for that matter. That night I was put in a situation where I didn't feel right and I had to make a hasty decision. Was it the right one? I'm not sure. But what I am sure of was on that awful night my life wasn't the only one that was in danger. It wasn't just about me anymore.

Everything about it is still so vivid, so crystal clear. So…haunting.

I reach up and feel my cheek. Just below my right eye, my fingertips follow the scar. It's still sensitive to touch, but it's healed. At least on the outside. As for the inside though, it'll take a long time—if ever—before the pain goes away. And even then I'm sure I'll never fully get over it.

I know over time it will get easier. Just in this last month, I've progressed tremendously. But I know the minute I see the face of my daughter, I'm going to be reminded again of him.

Brian. Brian Collins. My…my husband.

It could've been everything we'd wanted it to be. Our future was so promising. But something snapped and it didn't quite turn out the way we'd expected it. It just wasn't in the cards for us. I can push him far away in my mind and do my best to pretend it never happened, but the fact that we share a child together, is something that'll never go away.

The night I left had been one of the scariest of my life. I knew I had no other choice but to get away from him. The sooner the better. Surprisingly, when I'd demanded he leave, he actually did. I couldn't believe it.

I wish I'd been able to pack more of my personal belongings, but I didn't know how much time I had before he showed back up again. Thank goodness I kept all my important paperwork together. I moved quickly and grabbed what I felt was absolutely necessary. The rest of my things…well, they could be replaced. One thing was certain, I knew I never wanted to go back there again. Next time, I might not be so lucky.

That wasn't the first run-in I'd had with Brian. Just weeks prior, I'd agreed to accompany him to his hometown to meet his parents for the first time. I knew it was painful for him, that he'd had a lot of baggage he was still carrying, but I believed I could help him. After all, I was his wife. I wanted to support him and to offer him strength. Together, we could overcome anything.

We were a little more than halfway when the argument had started—all over a stupid text message. The disagreement between us had gotten so heated, that his driving had scared me—like literally scared me to death. At my demand, Brian had pulled off the side of the interstate. I got out of the car and began walking to the next exit. We were in the middle of nowhere, but it was the only thing I knew to do.

He hadn't given up so easily though. He kept driving until he found me, then caused a huge scene inside the restaurant I'd gone into. It was embarrassing, to say the least, but there again, I was scared and hadn't known what else to do.

Todd Williams, an innocent bystander that had been eating with his grandfather at the time, immediately came to my defense but not before Brian had made an even bigger ass of himself. He ended up leaving me there, hours from home. Todd, without any hesitation, offered to drive me back. I was a little hesitant at first, not wanting to involve anyone else in our dispute, but Todd insisted he didn't mind. Before Todd pulled away that night, he offered me his phone number. Not that he wanted me to call him or that he was trying to interfere, but to let me know I wasn't alone, that if I ever needed anything, he'd be there. If I ever needed to talk, he'd listen. It felt kind of strange such kindness coming from a complete stranger, but there was something about Todd, something that was comforting and genuine.

Over the course of a couple of weeks, things between Brian and I improved. It seemed we were back on track again. I still held my guard up, but I was willing to see my marriage succeed.

I never anticipated speaking with Todd again. I chalked it up to a good Samaritan being in the right place at the right time.

Brian and I pushed the incident aside, and I didn't bother to bring up Todd. Although he was a phone call away, I felt it best to move forward.

While at work one night, I decided to send Todd a text, thanking him for his kindness and generosity. Over the next several nights and countless texts later, we formed a friendship—if that's what you want to call it—just through our messages. It helped me to pass the time at work and it was a much needed break for him from his studying. Neither of us were looking for anything more. After all, I was married, but it felt good to connect with someone, to have a friend who didn't judge me.

Then, just a few nights later when the episode had happened between me and Brian, I called upon Todd for help. It was almost like he knew I'd need him again.

It was the middle of the night, but it hadn't mattered. True to his word, he and his father came to my rescue. They met me at an exit just off the interstate. He told me not to worry and that he'd figure something out. I could've made the drive to his place on my own or at least to the exit to meet, but he felt I was too upset to be driving alone for that many hours. And, well, with Brian a loose cannon, it just wasn't safe for me to be out on the highway alone.

I'm not sure why I chose to call Todd over my best friend or even my parents, but, looking back, I'm glad I did. I needed to get as far away from Brian as I possibly could, and, at that moment, it was the last place I suspected Brian would ever think to look for me.

I didn't know how long Brian would be gone after I'd told him to leave so it was crucial for me to get as much of my things out to my car. I figured the first place he'd go to look for me would be Rebecca's. I hated not giving her a head's up, but she could handle him. And if he gave her any trouble, that's what the cops were for.

Todd had wanted to keep me on the phone the entire time I drove, but I'd convinced him it wasn't necessary. He did call a couple times to check in with me though. When I noticed his familiar white pick-up truck turning into the parking lot at the gas station, my heart rate had accelerated. That was the moment I knew I was safe.

He wasted no time climbing down from the truck and running over to my car. Instead of asking me questions concerning the cut on my face, he wrapped his arms around me and just held me. I began to sob, and he embraced me tighter.

Even now, I remember his words so clearly.

"It's okay. I'm here to help you. He can't hurt you anymore."

I can only imagine what his dad must've thought as he watched us standing there in each other's arms. After all, we were still somewhat strangers even though it felt like so much more.

After what seemed like forever, Todd placed his hands on my shoulders and pushed me back just enough to look down at my face. "What the heck happened? You've got a pretty nasty cut there." While he didn't touch it, he tilted my head to the side and allowed the florescent light from the gas station to give him a better view.

I explained to him it wasn't as bad as it looked and that I was okay. Todd motioned for his dad to come over so he could make introductions. It was really awkward meeting his father under those circumstances. Just like grandfather, he was the kindest man.

"Hi Jennifer. I'm Rick Williams, but you can call me Rick. It's nice to meet you." Todd's dad extended his hand out to shake mine and I gladly accepted. His voice was very pleasant and welcoming. "Please know that Todd and I will do whatever we can to make sure you are safe."

"Thank you so much, Mr. Williams. I apologize for disturbing you so late at night." As soon as he let go of my hand, I brought it up to cover my face. I was embarrassed for anyone to see.

"I'm just glad we could help." Rick added.

Todd and his dad shared similar features--dark brown wavy hair, broad shoulders and olive skin tone. It was obvious they were father and son.

"We've got a guesthouse on our property you're more than welcome to stay in for as long as you need." Rick continued. "My wife, Beth, will have fresh linens ready for you by the time we get back. I'm sure you must be exhausted and in need of some rest."

"Please, don't put yourself through any trouble for me." I told them both.

"It's not any trouble at all," Rick quickly assured me. "Our family welcomes you."

Just hearing those words nearly choked me up.

Mr. Williams went inside the gas station and grabbed three cups of coffee for us. The gesture was nice, but I was already very much awake without the extra caffeine. The only thing the coffee did for me was add an extra stop down the road for a bathroom break.

When Todd was finished filling his truck with gas, his dad got inside and waited for us to get situated in my car. I buckled my seatbelt and looked over at him, hardly believing what had transpired over the last several hours. It was sad knowing that similar circumstances had brought us together once again.

I couldn't say anything for the longest time. Who knew what Brian was capable of next? The look on Todd's face assured me he understood my silence.

Soon, I'd have to make the dreaded phone call to my parents. There was so much I still hadn't told them—my marriage, the baby on the way, my walking out. It was too much to think about at the moment. I just hoped I could reach them first before they found out on their own, or worse, through someone else.

I was a little surprised Brian hadn't tried to call me yet. Maybe he was giving me some time. Maybe not. I just knew he wasn't one for giving up so easily.

We'd been on the road probably thirty minutes or so when Todd finally spoke. Fortunately, the nights we had spent texting and getting to know one another made the moment not quite so awkward. I still questioned why Todd had been put in my life, especially since I'd made such poor decisions before where Brian was concerned. Was I honestly worthy of Todd's friendship?

I watched the green mile marker signs, one by one, as we drove past them. I even found myself glancing in the mirror a time or two just to make sure no one was following us.

I cleared my throat then took a long deep breath. As I shared every vivid detail of what happened, I realized I'd been caught up in a fantasy world. My parents would be so disappointed to learn I'd been taken for a fool. The smart, loving woman they'd raised had let a fairytale take control over her life. The worst part, there was no happily ever after. It'd not been love at all, but merely lust. Lust of the cruelest kind. No one should ever have to experience the ups and downs I'd been put through the last couple of months. It was enough to drive any sane person crazy.

Todd listened carefully while I poured my heart out yet again.

"And there's something else I need to tell you." I turned my head to look out the window at the rising sun. I needed a moment to regain my composure. I reached into the glove box and pulled out a few napkins. The cut on my cheek began to sting from each salty tear that escaped my eyes. My poor decision making where Brian was concerned was one thing, but the pregnancy was a result of pure stupidity on my part. I knew better than to have unprotected sex.

Todd sensed my hesitation. "You okay?" He asked, his tone full of concern.

"I will be." I replied, nodding my head. "I'm pregnant."

The car went deathly silent for a moment.

"I didn't want to say anything, but I thought you looked a little… different from the first time we met." Todd said.

"Yeah, a few pounds heavier." I added, trying to make a joke out of it.

"No, I didn't mean it like that at all." He told me then reached over to take my hand in his. "I've always heard pregnant women have a certain glow about them."

I knew he was just trying to be nice. "It's okay. You can scold me all you want." I told him. "I deserve it. Besides, you can't possibly see me "glow", as you put it. It's been dark up until now."

"I'm sorry," he apologized. "I didn't mean it *that* way."

"It's just…what are my parents going to think?" I paused momentarily. "It's bad enough I've not told them I got married, but to throw in being pregnant too is just going to send them further into shock."

"From what you've told me about your family, I think they'll be pretty understanding."

I let out a deep breath. "I hope you're right."

"Jennifer, my family will do what they can to help you, but knowing them the way I do, they are going to encourage you to tell your parents as soon as possible. It's best for everyone that you get everything out in the open so that they can help you, too."

"I just can't believe I was so naive. That idiot used me. He took advantage of me, and I couldn't see through him. And not just once. He did it over and over again."

I leaned my head back against the headrest and closed my eyes. I just needed a few moments to contain my emotions.

Chapter 2

Jennifer

Present day

"JENNIFER."

I look around to find where the voice is coming from.

"Jennifer, are you okay?"

"Hmm?" I ask, completely unaware I was daydreaming.

Todd walks up the steps to the front porch and sits down in the chair beside me. "Don't you just love the view here?"

"Mmm, it's gorgeous," I reply. "It doesn't get much better than this." There's something about being here—it's so soothing and tranquil. Coming here was the best decision I could've ever made.

For the first week or so, I was scared to death to go out outside. I was worried sick Brian had somehow discovered where I was hiding. What if he was watching me from the edge of the woods? What if he was waiting for the right moment to come face to face again? So many what ifs...so many.

Todd assured me the noises I heard were coming from the birds and squirrels—not from Brian—and that my imagination was just getting a little carried away. It was easy for him to say, and I knew he meant well, but he hadn't been there when Brian had lost his temper, when he'd flung the bottle at me, when glass went flying everywhere. He hadn't seen the evil look in Brian's eyes while blood poured from my face.

"Jennifer?" I hear my name again.

"I'm so sorry." I apologize to Todd, realizing my mind has wondered away yet again.

"Are you nervous about your family coming?" he asks.

"I am, but, at the same time, I'm so excited to see them again. I owe a huge apology to them both. They did so much getting me set up in the apartment just after they retired. And now," I pause for a moment. "I've screwed all that up. I truly had it made."

Once everything was out in the open with my parents—my marriage, the baby on the way, putting college on hold—a huge weight lifted from my body. I could actually look at myself in the mirror again and not feel ashamed.

I'd put off calling them for a couple days until I was able to pull myself together. My mom got so upset she was unable to finish talking to me, leaving my dad to absorb everything on his own. He, too, got choked up but managed to hold himself together as best he could.

I can't say that I blame them for reacting the way they did, but there was no changing what had happened. We had to make the most of the situation at hand.

They were grateful Todd's family had offered to assist me—a total stranger—and we immediately made plans for them to come visit soon. The property was big enough for them to park their RV, and Rick and Beth Williams welcomed them to stay as long as they wanted. My parents also made some sort of financial arrangement with them to cover any expenses I might have while staying here. Funny thing, no one really spoke about how long that would be. It was sort of like an open-ended stay, and it made me feel more at ease, knowing there was no hurry to leave.

Since I'd put a big dent in my savings account assisting Brian with the purchase of his car as well as a few other things that had come up, I was thankful my parents were so willing to help financially again. Things had just happened so fast and I had obviously not been thinking clearly or logically where Brian was concerned.

I eventually got around to calling Rebecca, too. I apologized for having turned my phone off the first couple of days after disappearing, but after I told her how many times Brian had called and sent text messages, she said she completely understood and probably would've done the same thing, too. I know my whereabouts are safe with Rebecca, but Brian, on the other hand, would stop at nothing to find me.

I knew better than to think Brian wouldn't give up without a fight. His calls had started the following morning, right after I got here. Over and over, my phone rang. If it wasn't ringing, then the alert was going off signaling one of his texts. At first his messages were apologetic and full of concern. But as they continued all throughout the day—mind you with no response from me—it hadn't taken long for them to turn into hateful, vulgar words that literally made me sick to my stomach. Yeah, the old Brian was back. For twenty-four hours straight, he continuously called or send me texts until I finally shut the phone off. By not answering his calls or responding to his texts, he should've gotten the hint loud and clear—I didn't want to talk to him.

I had a long way to go to get my life straightened out again but I felt positive I'd made the right choice. Leaving Brian may have actually saved my life. Who knows what he was capable of—after all, I'd watched him deteriorate right before my very eyes. At least now I'm on the right track to getting my sanity back. That is until my phone rings…and I lose myself for a brief moment all over again.

I know I'll never go back there again. It's just too…too painful. It was so hard leaving my things behind—things that belonged to me, that I deserved to have with me again, but if it meant coming face to face with Brian again, well, I was willing to let them go.

The lease on the apartment is coming up for renewal in a couple weeks and Brian's really going to be surprised to find out he's not going to have a place to stay anymore. Since I never bothered to have his name added to the lease, he's pretty much screwed. He may have gotten lucky staying there rent free for a little while, but his luck is about to run out. The joke will be on him, though. Doesn't matter what kind of excuse he comes up with this time. Even though I never want to see or hear from him again, I can't help but wonder what he'll do when he finds out. Knowing him, he'll resort back to sleeping in his car again since that's the one thing he was good at.

I can't suppress the light chuckle that escapes my mouth just thinking about it.

"What's so funny?" Todd asks.

"Huh?" I turned my head to look at him, forgetting for a moment that he was beside me. "Oh nothing. Just thinking...about things." Then, I shake my head, realizing I know Brian pretty good. It's exactly what he would do.

As for the car I helped him get, well, I'm sure it's only a matter of time until the finance company picks it up. They're not going to let him drive it around without paying for it. I could kick myself for taking money out of my savings and also for adding my name to the loan. If I know Brian, he's still without a job. Whether it was me or his parents or that ex-girlfriend of his, seemed someone was always harping on him to work.

Something else that hadn't crossed my mind up until now—I never bothered to give Brian a key to the mailbox. I'm fairly certain, since he didn't have access, he hasn't paid the power bill either. I mean, why would he? It was one of the bills I took care of prior to him coming into my life. He never contributed towards it when he was working so why would he even consider paying it now. I hope to God he doesn't think I'm still going to pay it even though I'm not there. It's just the way he would think, though. Once the disconnect notice goes out, well, it's a matter of time until it's shut off. Poor guy, looks like he may be spending his last few days there in the dark.

Such a loser. I don't think I've ever met anyone who cared so little about themselves or had such a lack of determination.

I rub the spot on my finger where my wedding rings used to be. I took them off not long after getting here. I wrapped them tightly in a tissue and stored them in the side pocket of my suitcase that I stored underneath the bed. Just like the old saying, "out of sight, out of mind." I hadn't worn them long enough to have any kind of effect on me. Yet again, another hasty decision I'd made that backfired on me and, not to mention, another payment I'm sure Brian won't even think twice about.

"Todd, don't answer this," I sit up straight. "But what the hell was I thinking?"

"We all make mistakes, Jennifer. No one is perfect. You've got to stop blaming yourself. It's not healthy for you or the baby." He continues. "You've got to stop beating yourself up about this."

Todd has been the perfect gentleman this entire time. His parents, well, not only have they bent over backwards to make sure I'm content, but they remind me so much of my own. Just by putting in some additional mini blinds and adding a home security system, told me how much they cared. I admit I was uneasy coming here—God, I was terrified to death—but they've really helped me to overcome a lot of the nervousness I had in the beginning. It was tough being in a new place and not knowing anyone or my way around.

Rick and Beth had invited me over to eat dinner with them a couple of times that first week. We made small talk while we ate, and afterwards I helped Beth clear away the dishes. It was the least I could do. I was a little fearful being out after dark so I made a point of heading back to the guest house before it got too late.

Although I eventually warmed up to them, it was somewhat awkward, given the circumstances, with Todd not being around much the first few weeks. He was finishing up with his classes and had apologized like crazy for basically leaving me all alone.

One Friday we planned a trip into town. I needed to pick up a few groceries, and Todd wanted to show me a shortcut for getting off the mountain. At the time I didn't think I'd be venturing anywhere by myself any time soon, but it still didn't hurt to know.

We rented a couple of movies and he took me to the local library. I ended up with an armful of books as well as an access code to download books online, too. I was in heaven. I wasn't used to having so much time on my hands, and the books would keep my mind occupied. Also, I'd be able to read up on my pregnancy—something I hadn't really had the time to do.

It did get a little easier, though, as each week passed. By the end of the third week, I was sitting out on the front porch by myself listening to the sounds of nature and taking in the sheer beauty of everything around. That's not to say I didn't jump when a squirrel took off running after another squirrel through the tree branches, but there was just something about being here. Almost like the woods were protecting me instead of harboring something bad as I'd once thought.

The Williams' guest home has been perfect for me. There's just one bedroom but it reminds me so much of my apartment except that it's a house. Everything was already furnished, all the way down to the bathroom linens. Considering I left with just a few personal items, it's been nice not having to worry about the small stuff. I know I can't make this my home forever, but everything here is really starting to grow on me and I could get used to it. Except for being outside of the city, it'd be a perfect place to raise my baby.

The Williams' family purchased the property many years ago, back when Todd was just starting kindergarten. And now that he's finishing up with college, they're not in any hurry for him to leave. The guest home, on the other hand, is just a few years old. His parents had it built for his grandparents back when his grandmother became ill. The plans were to have them move here, making it easier on his mom who'd agreed to help take care of her. Sadly, though, the grandmother passed away before the move took place and the fully-furnished house remained unoccupied.

Todd's grandfather, whom I'd met that day when Todd had driven me to meet Rebecca, couldn't bear to leave the memories he still carried of his wife. I've noticed he comes to visit on a regular basis. The first time I spotted his car coming up the driveway, I'd panicked because it was the same color as Brian's.

The baby starts to move around, and I bring my hand up to place it on my belly. The flutters only last for a brief moment, but it's the most amazing feeling knowing a human being in growing inside.

I look over at Todd who's rubbing a spot on the armrest of the wooden rocker he's sitting in and ask, "How's your grandfather doing?" It's the first thing that comes to mind.

"Dad's invited him to come over this weekend. I know your parents are coming in but he figured it'd do him good to be around people."

Todd's schoolwork prevented him from spending a whole lot of time with his grandfather. I just hope now that he's out, he gets back into the routine of doing things with him instead of feeling obligated to be with me.

"He seems like a very sweet man."

"He's an amazing man. He's just so lonely without my grandmother. I'm going to take him to the flea market next

Saturday morning. You should join us. We'll be back in plenty of time before your folks get here."

"I wouldn't want to take away from your time with him," I quickly add.

"Seriously, he would love for you to come along. In fact, he suggested it."

"Well, I'll think about it." I love the idea of browsing a flea market, but I'd hate to be a burden on them.

"I'm not taking no for an answer. You stay here all day long and you need to get out more."

I can't help but smile. "If you insist."

"I wouldn't have asked if I didn't want you to."

"So, I've been thinking," I twist a strand of my hair in between my thumb and forefinger. "I'm going into town on Monday to return some books to the library. I thought while I was there I might see if any of the downtown businesses are doing any hiring."

"Are you sure you're up to working?" Todd asks.

"I'm not helpless," I tell him and immediately feel bad for the tone I used. "I didn't mean it that way. It's just I'm sure there's something I can still do. I've still got a little bit of time before the baby comes and health wise I'm doing just fine. Besides, the more active I am, the easier it will be for me when she's born."

"I guess you're right. As long as you're careful," he adds.

"And, I don't want to rely on my parents for everything. The little bit of money I have left in savings isn't going to last forever."

"Have you heard anything from Brian?" I can tell he regrets asking me this the moment the words have left his mouth.

Just hearing Brian's name sends goose bumps throughout my body. "He still calls my phone a couple of times each day—sometimes he leaves a message and sometimes he doesn't. I never answer, though. You should hear some of the messages he leaves. They're horrible."

"I'm sorry. I hate I even brought him up," he apologizes.

"If he'd just leave me alone," I tell him. "I need to make a decision about his cell phone. Even though I'm the one responsible for his phone since I was the one who added on his line, I'm also the one who can have it shut off at any time, too."

"I can only imagine how pissed he'd be about that. It is one way to put a stop to the phone calls, though."

"Yeah, it's something for me to think about. Among other things."

"Such as?"

"Well, right now, there's really nothing I can do until after the baby. My scholarship is on hold according to my advisor. I want to finish my degree, but not at that school. I won't go back there. I can't. I should be able to transfer everything once I come up with a plan. And, once I know where I'll be living." I look over at the confused expression on Todd's face.

"What do you mean, where you'll be living?" He questions my previous statement. "I thought you were content staying here."

"I love it here, I really do, but I can't expect your parents to let me stay forever. They've been kind enough already. Once I get back on my feet again after the baby is born then I'll start taking a better look at my options. What about you? What's your plans?"

"You had me worried there for a minute. I thought you were talking about leaving within the next couple of weeks." Todd's face relaxes. "It's hard to believe I'm almost finished with pharmacy school. With graduation just around the corner, it seems like just yesterday I was playing pee-wee football."

"I know your dad is looking forward to you joining him full-time at the pharmacy. He brought it up pretty regularly when we were having dinner. I bet it's been tough on him having the family business and not being able to take time off or take a vacation when he'd like."

"Funny you should mention that. He's already lined up a cruise for him and my mother in the fall. I just hope I pass all the state boards." He chuckles. "Or else, my dad's got to come up with a new plan."

"You're going to do just fine." I look over at him and smile. I feel the baby moving again and bring my hand up to rest on my stomach.

"You okay?" Todd asks, noticing my hand.

"The baby's just being very active this morning," I tell him. "Could be because I've not had anything to eat yet."

"Why don't you come down to the house for some breakfast then? I'm sure I can find something to make."

"Are you sure?" I ask. "I've already had dinner there a few times already this week. I'm becoming a permanent fixture at the table."

Todd stands up and offers his hand out to me. "Come on. I don't want to hear such nonsense. I told you that you're more than welcome to eat with us any time."

Chapter 3

Brian

MY PHONE RINGING STARTLES ME. I jump up from the swing on the patio and run inside. *Please, God, let it be her.* I make it to the table just as the ringing stops and watch the number fade from the screen. Sadly, it's one of those 1-800 numbers that's been blowing up my phone the last few days and not her.

Some days I call her just once. Then, there are other days I when I dial her number non-stop. Over and over, sometimes up to twenty or thirty times a day, hoping she'll give in and answer. I know I'm being ridiculous, but I just miss her so much.

I called the phone company just the other day to see if they could tell me the location of her phone. I made up some stupid story that we misplaced it while on vacation and would like to try and track it down before having it disconnected. Okay, I was desperate, but it was smart on my part to think of it. Since I'm not the primary account holder, though, they wouldn't release any information to me. Nothing. Nada. Not one single thing about the phone.

After hanging up, I got online and tried to reset the account password. I figured if I could see a detailed list of the calls she's made, the cell phone tower location might be there, too. Well, resetting it might would work but without her email password to retrieve the temporary new one, I was no better off than when I first thought of the idea. Damn it, I'm not giving up.

Last week there was a notice taped to the door saying it was time to renew the lease for the apartment. I panicked. Jennifer's parents had been the ones to take of this for her and I'm pretty sure by now they're aware of what's going on. And, if she's not planning on coming back—which seems to be the case—then I doubt there'll be a new lease to sign. What's going to happen to me? Where will I go? Will someone else move in?

So far, I've not had to worry about food. She must've just bought groceries right before she left because the cabinets and pantry was well-stocked. I've put a big dent in it and some of the main things like milk and Coke are all gone, but I've been able to find other things to drink.

Lucky for me, I caught the mailman before he dropped the mail into the slot. He recognized me from the time before and handed everything over without even thinking about it. Good thing I did, too. It happened to be the same day my last paycheck from the shoe store came in. I'd have been screwed without it. Rather than driving down to the bank to get it cashed, I walked to the grocery store down at the corner. I had to pay a fee just to get my money, but the bank would've charged me one, too. I swear, everyone's out to nickel and dime you for everything.

Other than a few outings, I've pretty much stayed here doing what I do best—watching TV and sleeping. I know it's not an exciting life and I can't do it forever, but I just keep hoping that one day she's going to walk in the door. We'll apologize to each other and everything will go back to the way it was.

I think about our baby that she's carrying, and I truly hope everything is okay with the pregnancy. I…I still can't believe I'm going to be a daddy.

I stopped by the hotel one afternoon to see if I could get any information out of Rebecca. She wouldn't admit much, but I could tell she'd been in contact with Jennifer just from the few things she said. It hadn't taken her long to start in on me about the money I still owed her, and I knew then it was time for me to leave. Fuck Rebecca and fuck the bracelet. Hell, I'll even give her the damn thing if she'll just shut the hell up about the money. Money, money, money. It's always about the money.

As soon as I got back to the apartment, I threw the bracelet across the room. I'd like to choke Rebecca with it. I knew she was holding back information about Jennifer, and it's not right. Jennifer is my wife, and I deserve to know what's going on.

Just thinking back to that day pisses me off. I realize I'm still holding onto my phone and I'm squeezing it so tight, my hand is now red. *Fuck my life.* I decide to send her another text. What's it going to hurt?

Me: Please call me. I need to know u r ok.

I hit send even though I know in the back of my mind the chances of her replying are slim to none.

I figure I've got about a month before I'll have to vacate the apartment. Surely they'll give some leeway if we're undecided about renewing the lease. I can make up some story, say she's out of town for a few weeks. Anything to bide some time.

I walk back out to the porch. It's almost too warm to sit out here anymore, but I still enjoy sitting in the swing. Jennifer and I had some really good times out here.

****

Knock, knock.

Not realizing I drifted off to sleep, I'm awakened by someone knocking on the door. I run inside and look through the peep hole before opening the door. Two men wearing some sort of work uniform are standing on the other side. One of them leans forward to knock again and I strain to read the stitched print right above his shirt pocket. *Tri-county Utilities.* What the...? Why would someone from there be here?

Then it hits me. The damn electric bill. Did Jennifer pay it before she left? Surely she did. She was always on top of stuff like that. But, even so, it's been a month now, and I'd be willing to bet they're here to collect the payment. How the fuck am I supposed to take care of it? Slowly, I slide my hand away from the doorknob. There's no way I'm answering the door now. Eventually the guys leave, and I release a deep breath. *Fuck!*

I sit down on the couch and flip on the television. I think of a couple excuses I can give them should they come back later on. The same one—she's out of town—pops into my mind. Or, what if I told them she's in the hospital. Yeah, that sounds even better.

As usual, a replay of one of last night's baseball games is on. I already know the outcome but leave it on anyways. Updates and times for the day's games scroll along the bottom of the screen, and I make a mental note of which ones I want to watch tonight. Then, all of a sudden, the television cuts off and the apartment is filled with silence.

I get up and go to the kitchen. What now?

The clock on the stove and microwave are dark—not one single neon light is on. I open the refrigerator door to complete darkness. Son of a bitch!

It doesn't take long before it hits me. The freaking power is off. This seriously can't be happening. I run my fingers through my hair and think of possible reasons why they might need to shut it off, ignoring the real reason that lingers in the back of my mind. Maybe the guys were here to let me know the power was going to be shut off temporarily because they were working on something. Sounds possible but I know it's not likely.

I walk over to the patio doors and pull back the blinds. The daylight brightens the room, but isn't going to do much good later on tonight once it gets dark outside. I rummage through some drawers in the kitchen hoping to find some candles or maybe even a flashlight. I check the pantry as well, but come up empty handed. There's got to be something around here I can use.

Next, I check the linen closet in the hallway and, thank goodness, find a couple of scented jar candles. I take a whiff of one. *Yuck!* It's one of those girly scented ones that smells like a fruit basket. What good is a candle, though, without having something to light it with? I rummage back through the drawers again and end up finding one of those long handled ones used to light grills and such. It'll work, but I hope this is just a temporary issue.

Since there's really nothing I can do for the time being, I go back out to the porch. I turn on my phone and open one of my favorite games. I collect my bonuses but even it's not holding my attention. For once, I'm worried about the situation at hand. Rather than draining the battery, I shut my phone off and slip it into my pocket. It's the smartest thing I've done in quite some time now.

It's roughly been an hour now since the power went out. Frustrated, I walk back inside, grab my keys, and head for the door. I need answers and I need them now.

I drive over to Rebecca's house and mentally try to prepare myself. Today, I'm not leaving until I have some information.

Rebecca's car is parked in the driveway, and I pull up behind it. *You can do this, Brian. Just remain calm.* By the time I make it to the porch, she's already standing there glaring at me.

"What do you want?" Rebecca asks. Her tone is the same as always with me—short and snide.

"I know you know where she is, Rebecca. You've known this entire time, and I'm not leaving until you tell me where my wife is. I need to know that she and my child are okay."

"And just who the hell do you think you are coming here demanding that I give you information about her?" Rebecca spats back.

"I am Jennifer's damn husband, that's who I am!" I shout. "I have a right to know her whereabouts."

Rebecca just stares at me blankly. I'd like to slap the...but I bite my tongue. *Don't lose your cool, Brian.*

"Come on, I need to know she's okay." I plead.

"I don't have to tell you anything. You should've thought about that before you acted like a damn crazy person, going off on her the way you did." Rebecca is not giving in one bit.

"That's where you're wrong. Had you kept your nose in *your* own business instead of mine, then none of this would've ever happened in the first place."

"I don't know what you're talking about, Brian."

"You know damn well what I'm talking about. You couldn't wait to pick up the phone to tell her you'd seen me out. It was my place to tell her I got fired, not yours." I grit my teeth, getting angry again just thinking about it. "It's your fault we had the argument in the first place that night. It's. Your. Fault." I emphasize that last part.

"Brian, I'm going to say this one time and one time only. Get out of my face. Leave my house and do not come back. I don't know where Jennifer is, and even if I did, you would be the last person I'd share that information with. Do you hear me?" Rebecca screams with her finger pointed in my face.

It takes everything in me to keep from slapping her. "You'll pay for this, bitch!" I threaten.

I turn and walk back to my car. I back from the driveway and as soon as I shift the car into drive, I slam my foot against the accelerator. A trail of smoke, the smell of burning rubber, and thick black marks are all I leave behind.

When I reach the stop sign at the end of the street, I reach up to wipe away a lonely tear that escapes. Why do I keep blaming everyone else for my shortcomings? Why can't I own up to my mistakes? It's no wonder Jennifer couldn't wait to get away from me—I'm…I'm a loser.

Chapter 4

Todd

I STOPPED BY TO VISIT Jennifer last night just to remind her about going into town to the flea market this morning. The last thing I want to do is bug her or get on her nerves for visiting so often, but she sincerely seemed excited about going. Not to mention, my grandfather was looking forward to having her join us, too.

I knock on the front door and wait for her to answer.

"Good morning." Jennifer opens the door and has a radiant look about her. Her smile looks so much better than the frown she'd worn for so long. "Right on time."

I'm one of those people who can't stand to be late, so I'm bad about arriving *too* early. I developed this punctuality from my parents—not that it's a bad habit to have but it's hard when not everyone else is the same way. "Please, take your time. Don't feel like I'm rushing you or anything," I assure her.

"No, I'm ready," she says. "Just let me grab my purse."

I notice Jennifer's outfit is one that I've not seen her wear before. It's a loose-fitted printed top that she's paired up with a pair of blue, denim-like shorts. It looks really cute on her. Even though there's still roughly three months left before the baby is expected, from what I can tell, she's managing her weight very well. I'm no pregnancy expert, but I think everyone else would agree—she looks great. Her top adds emphasis to her little baby bump and the color definitely brings out the blue in her eyes. I want to compliment her and tell her how cute she looks, but I'm not sure how she'd take it.

We walk side-by-side out to my truck. I reach up to open the door for her and offer my hand for assistance. I know it's the gentlemanly thing to do, but I sometimes find myself wanting to do things for her as though we are a couple. I won't deny, I wonder when people see us, if they think we're together. As in, you know, together. Like husband and wife or boyfriend and girlfriend.

In reality, I probably should've borrowed my mom's car so Jennifer wouldn't have such a difficult time getting in and out since the truck sits so high up off the ground, but she doesn't appear to mind at all. I close the door when she's in all the way and run around to my side.

"We've got time to stop and grab some breakfast if that's okay with you." I bring up as soon as I'm behind the wheel.

"That'd be great," she tells me. "Lately, I feel like I can't get enough to eat. I just eat and eat and eat. As that old saying goes, pretty soon, I'll be as big as a house."

"Well, you are eating for two now." We both laugh.

I have to admit; I still get kind of nervous being around her. We've established the importance of our friendship, but I can't help but wonder if one day there could possibly be more. She's definitely someone I'm attracted to, but now's not the time to even suggest anything like that. Besides, she's only separated from Brian and not divorced. That's the last thing I want to do—pursue a relationship with a married woman. My father would kill me!

Not long after Jennifer first got here and she'd somewhat gotten settled in, I stopped by one afternoon to visit with her. I felt bad for not spending any time with her that first week but I couldn't ignore my studies. I promised her I'd make it up to her, and so far, I've lived up to that promise.

A light rain had begun to fall so we sat out on the porch listening to the raindrops as they landed on the metal roof. We started talking about random things which eventually led to a serious conversation about relationships and how honesty and trust play a vital role in them. I decided to bring up how I'd made the decision to give up dating once I entered pharmacy school. I went on to explain to her how I wanted to be committed to school one hundred percent. I didn't want the distraction of having a girlfriend or just dating in general. Occasionally I'd hang out with the guys but even that didn't happen very often. All in all, I guess I wanted to show just how committed I was to my future. I didn't want to just live my life day to day with nothing to look back on. She said she completely understood and it made perfect sense to her, too. As she told me how proud she was for my accomplishments and achievements, she grabbed ahold of my hand. It...it meant something to me. I'm not sure what, but I felt the connection. I felt there was something about her, that we were a lot alike despite what she'd gone through.

We then talked about her degree and what her aspirations had been before having to put everything on hold. I discovered she'd been really sick in the beginning, even having to go to the hospital, which is how she found out she was pregnant. Her story wasn't an unusual one—it's happened to lots of young women—but I felt she was really determined to succeed. She was willing, somehow, to make it all work. Then, she said something that made me stop and think how fortunate I was to have the support of my parents. She told me she felt like she'd failed her own and that she was a big disappointment to them.

I truly felt bad for her even though that wasn't the case. Her parents still loved her just as much as they had before any of this happened. If Brian had been more of a husband and was supportive and dedicated to their marriage like he should've been, then she could've worked towards those dreams instead of being ashamed of them. Outwardly, she appears stable but I know inside she's still a basket case. I see how she constantly looks around; I notice she jumps as the slightest sounds. It's just not right. After all this time, she's still living in fear.

I knew it was definitely over between the two of them when she told me she'd been in touch with an attorney. She wanted to divorce him as quickly as possible. As long as Brian was still staying at the apartment, it was easier to track him down. Once he's evicted, though, the process might take longer and serving him papers would be even more difficult. It made perfect sense, especially coming from her. She realized what was at stake. It was also one of the reasons why she hadn't had his cell phone disconnected yet. Once it's turned off, who knows where he'll go or what he'll try then.

Her situation is so heartbreaking. How can one human being be so damn cruel? I don't doubt any of the stories she's told me about him, but it's almost impossible to fathom that one individual can make someone else's life so miserable just because they can't grow up and accept some responsibility.

She's lucky she got away from him when she did. From all she's told me, it was only a matter of time until Brian got worse, until his temper and mood swings got even further out of control. In my book, that's just not okay—not for anyone.

Jennifer told me she didn't want to pursue another relationship for a very long time, and I can't say that I blame her, especially since she's had to endure so much with Brian. But I hope once she gets everything situated, she'll think differently. I'm not saying she won't be a good parent, but it's not going to be easy for her to play both parent roles for her daughter once she gets older. Then, she really took me by surprise. She said that when she did decide to start dating again, she hoped she'd fine someone like me—hard working and dedicated.

I had to stop and ask myself was it possible I had a slight crush on her? Maybe? Had it happened and I not even realized it?

Right now, neither of us are in the position to even think about that. I'm enjoying her friendship, no doubt, but I will admit, if we were in a different point in our lives, she's definitely someone I could see myself dating. And, the fact she's having a baby doesn't really matter because I know the circumstances.

I sigh just thinking about it all. I've been single for so long now, when the time does come for me to start dating again, I just hope she's still in the picture.

I think my dad sensed how much I'd started to care for her, too, and he asked me if there was anything he needed to know about. I've always had a great relationship with him and I wasn't about to ruin it by not being honest with him. I explained to him she'd started working on her divorce, but, other than that, we were just friends and nothing more. He told me he was proud of me for supporting her because, right now, she needed a friend more than anything.

"Todd?" She calls out my name and I snap out of the daydream I was having.

"Sorry, I was just thinking about something." I tell her, not wanting to admit that *she* was the "something" I was thinking about. "I hope you're hungry. The place we're going to has the best breakfast."

"You know, I always helped get the breakfast ready at work. We didn't actually cook anything but the Danishes and muffins we served were pretty darn good. I, uh, sort of had a bad habit of bringing them home with me."

I pull in to Reese and Paula's, a locally-owned mom and pop restaurant, and squeeze the truck in a parking spot towards the rear. It's busy for a Saturday morning. I'm barely stepping out of the truck before Jennifer walks up to me. I can't help but laugh out loud.

"What?" she asks. "Do I have something on me?"

"No, not at all. The way you jumped out of my truck, you'd think you were starving."

I notice a few people look up at us when we walk in—probably wondering who the young lady is that's accompanying me. I try not to let the stares bother me, but I'm sure it won't take long before word gets around that I was having breakfast with a pregnant, pretty young lady. That's the price you pay for living in a small town all of your life—where everyone knows everything about you—but I wouldn't want to live anywhere else.

The hostess greets us with a smile and takes us to an available booth towards the back. Jennifer slides in on one side and I take the side that faces the front. Anyone coming in is sure to see her, and not my parents, that I'm having breakfast with.

I watch Jennifer glance around the restaurant before picking up her menu. I know exactly *who* she's looking for.

"You don't have to worry," I tell her and place my hand on top of hers. "He's not going to find you here."

"I know, but it's just something I can't take any chances with. It's been a few days now since he's called and that's not normal for him."

"Have you thought about contacting the police?" I ask. I realize I'm rubbing my thumb over her silky smooth skin and I quickly stop, hoping she doesn't notice. I can't believe I was so oblivious to doing it. It just felt…it felt so natural.

"I have but I don't know if there's anything they can really do about it. They'll probably just tell me to have my number changed or, better yet, just have *his* phone shut off."

"Yeah, perhaps you're right." I hate our conversation has turned to the subject of Brian again. "Have you had a chance to look at the menu yet?"

"What do you recommend besides the pancakes?" Jennifer asks, accepting my suggestion to change the subject.

"I've tried pretty much everything and it's all good," I tell her. "But the pancakes are my favorite. They even bring you heated syrup to go with them."

"Hi, guys. What can I get you both to drink this morning?" Our waitress interrupts. I recognize her as the younger sister of a guy I graduated high school with.

"Um, I think I'll have apple juice," Jennifer tells her.

"And I'll have milk, please." I add.

"Will this be on one ticket?" the waitress asks.

"Yes," I quickly add.

"I can take care of mine," Jennifer says, but there's no way I'd let that happen.

"It'll be one." I confirm.

"And do we need more time or do you know what you'd like?"

Even though I know what I want, Jennifer's still looking over the menu.

"Babe, do you need more time?" I ask.

"No, I'm good. I'll have a small stack of your pancakes with an order of bacon please." She tells the waitress, her cheeks slightly flushed.

"And I'll have the same." I tell her and hand both our menus to the waitress. "Are you okay?"

We both look up at the same time, neither of us knowing what to say. I look away when I feel my own face redden. She reaches for her purse and runs her fingers along the strap nervously.

"I'm sorry about that," I offer an apology before she's able to say anything.

"Sorry for what?" she says without looking at me directly.

"I...I didn't mean to call you babe." I'm totally at a loss for words, almost like we're on a first date.

"It's...no big deal. Really, it's okay." She then says, "I've just not had anyone call me that before."

Almost instantly, we both look up, and our gazes lock together.

The waitress returns with our drinks at the right moment. "Here you go," she says and sets them down in front of us. "Can I get you both anything else while we're waiting on your food?"

"I think we're good," I reply.

Just as our waitress is about to walk away, one of the other servers walks up behind her holding two plates.

"Well, what do you know. Just in time," she tells us, then, one at a time, places them in front of us.

Jennifer reaches for her silverware. "Man, you weren't kidding. This looks delicious."

Between the two of us, we use most all the syrup. Neither of us say very much while we eat.

"I wasn't lying when I told you it was good, huh?" I mention just as she forks the last bit of pancake into her mouth.

"We've got to come back here again," she says with a satisfied expression on her face. "These pancakes have been out of this world. I'd like to try one of the breakfast casseroles next time. They sounded really good."

"I like that idea," I add. "A lot." I glance down at my watch and notice the time. If we're going to make it to my grandfather's house by nine, we need to be leaving soon. I can see him now, standing at the front door with his hands on his hips.

The waitress clears our plates then drops off the ticket. "You can just take care of that up front."

"This was pretty good. How about next time it's on me. Deal?" Jennifer says while standing up from her seat.

"Sounds like a plan to me."

Minutes later, we're on our way again.

****

We spend the next couple of hours browsing the grounds of the flea market. There are always so many neat and exciting things to see. The only thing Jennifer buys is a few used paperback books. I know she visits the library quite often and I've even seen her with a reading device of some sort, but she says there's nothing better than having a real book in your hands. She's a true book addict, which I guess isn't a bad habit to have. I purchase a bag full of fresh vegetables for my mom. Many of the local farmers set up their booths here with the freshest, best-tasting vegetables that are ten times better than any you'd purchase at the supermarket. I also pick up a watermelon right before we get ready to leave. There's no way I could've carried it the entire time. The seller informs me it's the first crop of the season and they've been very sweet and juicy.

My grandfather, on the other hand, has both arms loaded down with his purchases. In one paper sack, he has an assortment of tools, nothing of extreme importance, just tools he claims are rare and hard to find. His garage/workshop at home is jam-packed with overflowing toolboxes so I find it hard to believe he doesn't already have one of everything. Still, he loves adding to his collection, and I hate knowing that one day someone is going to have to sort through everything when he passes away.

He also picked out a leather belt from a vendor. He claimed the one he has now is a little worn, but I have to wonder how truthful he's being. I don't say anything, but the new belt has "Paw-Paw" engrained into the leather. It's odd that he selects that particular one since all of his grandchildren are older now. I know Jennifer has visited with him when he's been over at my parent's house and he's also stopped by to check on her at her place a time or two. Just the other day he mentioned to me that "he sure had taken a liking to that girl." It makes me wonder if the "Paw-Paw" on the belt has any correlation to Jennifer's baby.

And another interesting purchase he made was six bottles of foot cream that an Avon vendor was selling. I had to keep from laughing but he was so serious when he told Jennifer and me how important it is to take care of your feet.

When we get back to the truck, he pulls two bottles of the cream out and passes one over to each of us. Jennifer and I look at each other, and it takes all we can do not to burst out laughing.

We finish up at the flea market just after lunch and drop my grandfather off at his house. Jennifer uses the restroom while I help him carry his bags to the garage. I notice over in the corner several pieces of wood he's been carving on and there's also something with a sheet draped over it.

"What's that?" I ask, pointing to the sheet.

My grandfather stutters as though caught off guard. "Oh, it's just a little something I've been working on. Nothing special."

"You and your projects." I laugh under my breath and shake my head. "I guess you can use some of your *new* tools to work on it, huh?" He knows I'm just picking on him.

"You'll see. Once I reveal my masterpiece you'll be sorry you didn't think of it yourself."

He follows me out to the truck at the same time Jennifer walks up. She reaches over to give him a hug.

"It's been fun, but I'm exhausted," I announce to them both. "I could sure use a nap right about now."

"I like that idea," my grandfather agrees. "I might just do that."

"Just don't forget about dinner tonight," I remind him. I would've said something about Jennifer's parents being there, too, but I know she's already nervous about seeing them.

"You bet'cha. I'll see you two later on this evening." He turns to walk inside then gives us both a wave before he shuts the door behind him.

Neither of us say a whole lot on the way home. So far the day has been perfect and I only hope the rest of it is that way, too. I drop her off at the guest house and thank her for coming along.

"I had a really great time with you and your grandfather. He's something else," she says.

I smile and nod my head. "He's a mess, that's for sure."

"We'll have to go back again. They had a lot of really neat things there."

"Well, I think I'm going to take that nap. Oh, and I might even use some of that foot cream afterwards."

"Oh, I almost forgot mine," she says with the most gorgeous smile on her face.

She shuts the truck door, and I wait until she's opened the front door before I pull away.

Chapter 5

Jennifer

I WALK INSIDE, LOCK THE door, then lean back against it. I take a deep breath and look around at everything. Nothing seems to be moved or out of placed—everything still looks the same. Call me crazy or whatever, but I've gotten into the habit, anytime I go somewhere, of leaving a book directly along the edge of the coffee table. Or, I've turned one of the pillows on the couch upside down. Silly, I know, but I'm still terrified to death Brian's going to find me. I'm afraid that one day I'm going to walk in and find him sitting on the couch waiting for me.

I read once that people don't think about putting things back in the exact same spot when they're looking for something. By leaving these items a certain way, I'd know immediately if they'd been moved.

I'd never admit it to Todd, but I felt like everywhere I turned today Brian was watching me. There were just so many people, Brian could've easily been amongst them. He could've lagged behind a couple feet and I would've never known it. I shudder just thinking about it, and I have to wonder if I'll ever get beyond feeling this way. Will I ever feel normal again?

I drop the books I bought down on the kitchen table then pour myself a glass of lemonade. Surprisingly, I'm not all that hungry, but my throat is parched. I didn't do anything strenuous today, but being out in the heat for those couple of hours really drained me. I take another swallow then sit down at the table for a few minutes.

I pick up one of my new books and read the back cover again. I'm so glad I picked this one up because it sounds so good. I think about starting it, but I know if I do, I might as well forget taking that nap.

I pull my phone from my purse to check the time and notice I have a couple of missed texts. *Please, God, don't let them be from him.* My stomach clenches and suddenly I have a hard time catching my breath. *Breathe, Jennifer. Just take a deep breath. It's not from who you think it is.*

I click on the message box, and sure enough, there's one from Brian as well as one from Rebecca and my parents. I literally want to throw the phone across the room but I realize that's something Brian would do. I'm better than that. I shouldn't let something like a stupid text from him get to me this way. He's Lord knows where, and I'm safe and sound here. He can't hurt me.

I check the one from my parents first. They're running a little behind schedule but should still get here in plenty of time for dinner. It'll be so good to finally see them again. I just hope I don't put them into a state of shock when they see me and how I've changed—my little pudge is not so easy to hide anymore.

I bring my free hand up to press my shirt against my belly—just to feel how my body has transformed—and nearly drop my phone. As I grab a hold of it, my fingers brush over the screen and one of the other messages pops up. Without thinking, I look down. Almost immediately my hands begin to tremble.

Brian: You need to call me asap.

Brian: I know U R ignoring me but you need to call me NOW!

The messages are no different than any of the others he's sent before. The next one upsets me so much, I start to feel like I'm going to pass out. I go to the refrigerator and refill my glass figuring something cold to drink might help me overcome this sudden spell. This can't be happening.

Brian: Bitch, I know U R home. Answer your fucking texts.

I break out in a sweat and contemplate calling Todd. *No, I tell myself, this is just another one of his ploys to upset me. I can't let him get to me.*

I go into the living room and double check the locks on the door and the two front windows. I can't believe I'm falling into his trap. This is exactly what he wants me to do do—worry!

I didn't waste any time contacting an attorney right after I came here and one of the first things he told me was no matter what kind of message he sends or leaves on voicemail, do not respond. Well, that's easy for him to say—he's not the one feeling threatened. According to him, any kind of contact—

even if it's not nice on my part—will only give him false hope. But if I just keep ignoring them, the conversations are only one-sided and he can't misinterpret my words.

Brian: Did you enjoy your day? Call me please.

The messages just keep coming. *Oh, God, he knows I'm here.* This can't be. *He's only playing mind games with me,* I tell myself. There's no way he knows my whereabouts.

Just when I'm at my breaking point and about to lose it, I type out "LEAVE ME ALONE!!" and press send.

Almost instantly, my phone *dings*. I force myself to look at the screen.

Rebecca: What is going on? Please tell me that text was not meant for me and that you are okay.

Relief washes over me. Rebecca. Oh, how I needed to hear from her.

Me: OMG. I'm so sorry. I thought your text was from Brian. He's at it again.

Rebecca: I miss you and have been worried about you. Is everything OK?

Me: I'm fine. Just a little stressed. Mom and dad arriving shortly. Having dinner tonight.

Rebecca: Tell them I said hello. I miss them.

Me: Sorry about that text.

Rebecca: No worries. B stopped by my house. Same crap as always. Thinks I'm going to tell him where you are, but he's wrong. Lips are sealed.

Me: Thank you. Sorry he won't leave u alone.

Rebecca: He will eventually. I hope. He just can't get the big picture can he?

Me: Lease up end of month. He'll know then.

Rebecca: Good for you. I miss you u.

Me: Miss you too. Let's talk soon.

Rebecca: Sounds good. Take care.

We say our goodbyes, and I realize the messages from Brian have stopped. I sure do miss my best friend and hate it came down to this. What other choice did I have though? I'd give anything to spend some time with her—maybe a weekend or something—but I can't afford to take the risk right now. There's no way for me to know if Brian is watching her every move, hoping she'll slip up and lead him straight to me. Nothing would surprise me about him at this point. He's desperate to find me any way he can.

I slip my shoes off and walk into the bedroom. I close the blinds but not before double checking to make sure the window is secured. *You're being paranoid for no reason, Jennifer.* I try to get comfortable on the bed but find myself tossing and turning, unable to relax. I shift the pillows, even crawling underneath the covers.

Finally, after what seems like forever, I drift off into a deep sleep. Instead of relaxing, my mind enters into a very vivid and disturbing dream.

Brian and I are back in my apartment. It's the same night he threw the glass bottle across the room. I'm begging and pleading with him to please put it down. No matter how much I try and convince him, he still gleams at me with a look of pure hatred. He swings the bottle back and forth, threatening me with it. It's almost as though he's...he's planning to throw it at me. He mutters something about Rebecca, something she supposedly said. I'm confused....

"No! No! Please don't," I scream. "No, Brian. I've not talked to Rebecca. I don't know what you're talking about. No! NOOO!"

I feel a warm hand on my shoulder and I jump, uncertain what the heck is going on. I'm confused and not sure where I am. As I gain focus through the tears that sting my eyes, I see Todd sitting beside me on the edge of the bed. He reaches up to push my matted hair away from my face.

"*Shhh*, baby, it's alright. He's not going to hurt you. You're safe here."

"What? What do you mean?" My words come out muffled and I realize I'm trembling.

As I try to sit up, Todd pulls me towards him and wraps his arms around me. The only thing I know to do is rest my head on his shoulder and let him embrace me.

"How did you get in?" I manage to ask. As soon as my words come out, I realize it's a silly question. Of course he's got a key to his family's place.

"I knocked a couple times, and when you didn't answer, I tried your phone. I started getting concerned—something didn't feel right—so I decided to use the spare key to let myself in. Good thing I did."

"I'm so embarrassed for you to see me like this." I reach up and wipe my face with the palms of my hands.

"Please, don't feel bad. I'm just glad I got here when I did." His voice sounds so sweet and sincere. "I hate seeing you upset. Did something happen?"

"Thank you, Todd. My dream was so real."

"Can I get you something to drink? Maybe some water?"

"That'd be great." I nod my head, then look down at the disheveled bed covers. They're all over the place, almost like a bunch of little kids spent the last hour bouncing up and down on them.

I make my way into the kitchen behind him and lean back against the counter.

"I'm sorry for startling you," He apologizes again. "I just didn't know what to do."

I drop my head down not sure what to say.

"How often does this happen? I mean, the dreams." He asks then lifts my chin with his finger so that I'm looking at him again.

I walk to the window and stare out. After a few moments, I turn back to face him. "The first week or so after I got here I had a hard time going to bed at night. I was lucky if I got an hour or two of sleep. Thank goodness I had all those library books or I would probably have lost my mind. I was just so afraid if I fell asleep he was going to come in on me. And when I would drift off, it'd only be for a little bit."

"Have you thought about talking to someone about this?" Todd suggests.

"I actually have a doctor's appointment next week. It'll be my first time meeting with her so I'm sure she'll have a bunch of paperwork she'll need me to fill out," I tell him. "It'll be a good time to bring it up."

When I first made the appointment, I briefly told the receptionist about suddenly having to leave my hometown for extreme personal reasons. I didn't want to go into too much detail on the phone and she assured me that anything I shared with them was protected under the laws of patient confidentiality. It was a relief to know that, but just thinking about having to tell someone what had happened concerned me. What if they reported it to the police? Would I have to go back and make a statement?

"I wish I could tell you everything's going to be fine, but you're headed in the right direction. Just stay strong and keep your head up," Todd reassures me. "You have my word I'll do whatever I can to make you feel safe."

"I hope you're right. And thanks."

"If the dreams continue, I can always come by when I get home from school at night. I can sleep on the couch and be gone before you get up in the morning."

"I couldn't ask you to do that for me. You already struggle as it is getting enough rest yourself." I'm shocked from his offer.

"Promise me you'll at least think about it, okay?"

I nod my head. "Alright, I will."

I catch a glimpse of a vehicle turning into the drive and my face lights up.

"Looks like someone's got company." He tells me.

"Look at me, I'm a mess." I say, pointing at my face and wrinkled clothes.

"Why don't you go freshen up, and I'll go down to meet them. I'll let them know you'll be down shortly."

"Todd, thank you. Thank you for everything." I reach up to give him a hug and hold onto him probably a little longer than I should.

Chapter 6

Brian

WELL, HERE IT IS, ANOTHER night of being in the dark. I still can't freaking believe the electricity was shut off; I guess, though, it was bound to happen sooner or later. Suddenly, it hits me—she's…she's not coming back. If she cared, she wouldn't have let his happen.

I walk back inside and pull the screen door shut on the sliding glass doors. I can only stay outside on the porch for so long before the mosquitos start to attack me. There's no air circulating at all inside the apartment and it's stifling. It's absolutely miserable. I wonder how people survived years ago without air conditioning? It'd be somewhat bearable if I had a fan but what good is a fan right now with no electricity.

Earlier today, I tossed out everything that was left in the refrigerator. I knew if I didn't do is soon, it was bound to start smelling bad and I don't think I could've handled the odor.

There's not much left to burn on the candles, either. They're not something I have to have, but it sure beats sitting in total darkness. And when I have to go to the bathroom, well, I just use the lighter to lead the way.

Occasionally I hear muffled voices coming from the other tenants—some outside in the hallway and some from the unit above. I wonder what they'd think if they knew I was in here, sitting alone in the dark. Would it freak them out to discover this about their neighbor? Or, would it even matter?

Being alone like this, I've had lots of time to think. The one thing I can't get off my mind, though, is food. Nor can I ignore the rumbling going on in my stomach. I'm barely scraping by with what's left in the cabinets, and sooner or later, I've got to come up with a plan. I've resorted to drinking water from the sink, and I almost gag when I swallow it. I'd give anything right now for an ice cold soft drink or, better yet, a beer. My mouth waters just thinking about it.

It hasn't been so bad taking cold showers, which I try to do mid-day when the temperature is at its hottest. I also skip a day, too, since I'm really not doing anything to get dirty. I've gotten into the habit of wearing my clothes for several days in a row. Since I can't wash anything in the washing machine, I'm having to rinse my stuff out in the sink. Talk about uncomfortable—jeans and underwear don't feel the same when they've had to hang dry.

I'm literally going crazy and I'm bored out of my mind. I wonder if this is what a person feels like who's in a care facility, left abandoned by their family and loved ones. Every day is the same, no visitors, no nothing. It's the same blank walls and no human interaction.

I did find a deck of cards in one of the kitchen drawers but the only thing I can really do with them is play Solitaire. It was okay at first, but I'm reaching that point where I'm considering playing something else, like Fifty-Two Pickup. I think we all learned how to play that one at some point in our lives. I swear if I never see another deck of cards again…

I also came across a stack of crossword puzzle books and the other kind where you search for the words then circle them. I guess Jennifer would take them with her to work at night. I learned really quick that I sucked at crossword puzzles. Heck, I couldn't even come close to getting all the answers right and it wasn't any fun flipping to the back. So I stuck with the word search puzzles. They were more my style. I've already done over half of one book, and I'm on my second ink pen. Either I've been really busy or they don't put as much ink inside them like they used to.

I got so bored the other day I decided to take a ride. Since I was almost out of gas, I sort of "borrowed" a can of gas from the maintenance guy's truck. If I'd been able to find him I would've told him some ridiculous story about running out of gas and being late for work, but since he was nowhere to be found, I said the hell with it and just took it. There were six other containers so I really doubt he'll miss it. Just to be on the safe side, I tossed the gas can in the backseat and drove down the road a little way. I pulled off in a parking lot then added the gas to my tank. It managed to bring the gas hand up to a quarter of a tank. It wasn't much, but it was more than I had to begin with and I could get around town for a few days before my fuel light would come on again. I threw the empty jug in a dumpster, but now I wish I'd kept it. Not that I was planning to run out of gas or anything, but you never know. Oh well, it was easy enough to take that one so I'm fairly certain I could swipe another one if I had to.

While I was out, I stopped by a few fast food places and inquired about a job. Yeah, can you believe it? I actually put forth an effort to find employment. It's not exactly the type of work I want to do, but right now, I'm starting to get a little desperate and…even a little scared. Money just isn't going to fall from the sky.

I discovered no one does paper applications anymore which totally sucks for me since I don't have a computer. I could use my phone to access the job websites to apply, but come on, it's almost impossible to read the small print and fill in all of the information correctly. One of the places suggested I use the public library since they had computers for public use, and I wondered why I hadn't thought of that myself.

So far I've been pretty lucky with keeping my phone charged using an outlet I discovered behind the stairs leading up to the second level of apartments. I'm a little hesitant to leave it there for any length of time should someone wonder by and see it. If something happened to my phone I'm not sure what I would do.

I decide to get out for a little while and do something for a change—I'm sick of staring at the walls. I throw on a baseball cap to cover up my hair but it doesn't help much. It's been so long since I've had a haircut, I'm considering taking the scissors to it myself. Not sure what kind of job I'll do on it, but it can't be much worse than what it is now.

Without giving it much thought, I drive over to the library. I used to think Jennifer was crazy for reading all the time, but the place isn't half bad. I grab a handful of magazines and head over to one of the tables in the back corner. Before I sit down though, I notice a section of books labeled mystery and thrillers. I've never cared much for reading, but some of these covers are incredible. I select a few of them and bring them to the table with me.

After an hour or so, I realize I'm just about halfway into this particular story and I'm dying to know how it ends. I notice someone shelving books so I ask them how to go about getting a library card. In a matter of minutes, I'm hooked up with one. I pick out a few more stories by the same author and place them on the counter. The cute young girl working the desk slips a bookmark inside one of them, and I smile and thank her.

As I walk out to my car, I notice the sky has darkened and it looks like rain could come down at any moment. I'm so eager to get back to the apartment to pick up where I left off but I know that if it starts to rain, it'll be nearly impossible to see. I might be able to sit out on the porch, but it wouldn't be for very long. Being on the back side of the unit, the trees don't allow much light to shine through. On a brighter note though, if it does end up raining, at least the temperature inside the apartment will be cooler. These last few nights have been unbearably hot.

I toss the books over in the passenger seat and crank the car. The wind has picked up and the trees are swaying back and forth. No doubt, it's going to pour. I blast the air conditioning on high and change radio stations before shifting the car into reverse. Without looking, I slowly start to back out.

Bam!

I snatch the gear shift back into park and slap the stirring wheel. *Fuck!* I open the car door and climb out, scared to see what I've hit.

Parked just off the shoulder of the road is a truck with a trailer loaded down with lawn equipment. As I walk around to inspect the damage, I see a gentleman walk outside from the building across the street and head my way. He stops to look at my car first, then glances over at his.

"You okay?" he asks.

"Yeah, I think so," I tell him, trying not to reveal how mad I am at myself. How could I even think of backing out into the street without checking to see if it was clear? What the hell was I thinking?

We both walk over to inspect his trailer. Surprisingly, the trailer looks fine, but my car didn't get off quite so lucky. There's a big dent in the right quarter panel and my taillight is busted. I know, it could be worse, but I've only had my car for a few months.

"Well, look. I know your car suffered more damage than my trailer, but I'm good with not calling the cops if you are," the other guy suggests.

I pull my cap off and run my fingers through my hair. "Yeah, I suppose you're right," I mumble. "I'm, uh, sort of between jobs right now, so I've kind of let my insurance lapse." I might be doing more harm than good by telling him this little bit of information, but with or without insurance, he had a point. The damage on his end was minimal.

"I hate to hear you don't have any insurance, but maybe someone can cut you a deal for repairs. It's really not that bad," he says as he brushes his hand over the dent. "Just get it popped out right here. Maybe some touch-up paint."

"Yea, but I've only had the car a couple of months. It stinks, you know. Proud of your new ride, then this."

"You said you were in between jobs, huh?" he inquires. "What kind of work you looking for? My brother and I have our own lawn care business, but he's been having to take off a lot to tend to his sick wife. We've got a pretty good client base but it's tough trying to keep up with everything all by myself. Sound like something you might be interested in?"

"Other than taking care of the grass when I was still a kid, I don't know too much about mowers and trimmers. But I'm sure I could learn." I tell him. "Are you offering me a job?"

I pause for a moment to really think about this job thing. As bad as I need one, do I really want to work outdoors getting hot and sweaty? Not to mention, dirty.

"Tell you what. Here's my card and if you change your mind, give me a holler. I know I just sort of sprung it on you, but I like to get started as early as possible in the mornings to beat the heat. I've got three jobs lined up for tomorrow and could sure use the help. My address is on the card. If you show up at six-thirty, it'll make my day. As far as this goes," he turns around and points to our vehicles. "We'll just let this little incident go and not hold anyone responsible. Deal?"

I take the card from him and scan it. **Doug and Gene's Lawn Care.**

"So, are you Doug or Gene?" I ask.

"I'm Doug. Doug Young." He extends his hand to me. "Sorry I didn't introduce myself earlier."

"Well, Doug, since you're in need of some help, and I'm in need of a job, six-thirty tomorrow morning sounds good to me."

A clap of thunder sounds followed by a sharp streak of lightening. "Heck yeah. You got yourself a job." He firmly pats me on the shoulder. "But if we don't get going now, we're going to get soaked."

No sooner than I get back in behind the wheel, the rain starts. It's coming down so hard, I'm tempted to sit here for a moment. I watch as Doug pulls away, the trailer lights hardly visible through the torrential downpour. I glance over at my stack of books. So much for reading them later on.

****

The rain is still coming down pretty hard when I make it back home. I look around inside my car for something to put my books in. I don't mind getting wet, but I know I should protect them as much as possible.

I spot a plastic bag from the floorboard and dump the contents out. An empty soft drink bottle and a crumpled chip bag fall to the floor. I'd give anything right now just to munch on some chips. My mouth waters just thinking about it. I promised myself I'd take better care of this car, especially with keeping the inside clean, but it didn't take me long to resort back to my old habits. Just look at it. I should be ashamed at the amount of trash that has accumulated.

Securing the books inside the bag, I make a mad dash for the apartment. I shake off the rainwater and sit the bag down on the ground next to the door. While I fish in my pocket for the keys, I notice a piece of paper tucked inside the edge of the door. I wonder who's been by to see me. I notice the word "Sheriff" before anything else as I unfold the paper. *Fuck!* As I scan over it, my body goes weak.

"This message is for Brian Collins. Please call Sheriff Timothy Jones at your earliest convenience. 555-3100 ext. 145."

I drop the bag of books down on the couch, my interest no longer on finishing my story from earlier. I reread the message again. I don't even want to think about why I need to call this sheriff. As if my day couldn't get any worse.

Since there's no reason to put it off, I turn on my phone and punch in the number. Suddenly, it occurs to me that maybe Doug changed his mind about the accident. What if he reported me for having no insurance? Or worse, what if he says it was a hit and run?

The more I think about it, I realize I'm crazy for even thinking that. There's no way the sheriff would've had time to talk to Doug, make a report, then drive all the way over here to talk to me. It's just not possible. I begin to fear the worse.

"Jones speaking." The voice is sharp and direct, almost like a military drill sergeant.

"Yes, I, uh, had a note left on my door stating I needed to call this number. Can you tell me what this pertains to?" I try to sound calm my but palms are sweaty and I'm having a hard time catching my breath.

After I've verified myself, the sheriff informs me he has important paperwork that needs to be hand delivered. My body tenses and a sheen of sweat covers my body. Paperwork? I can't imagine who'd be sending me paperwork that needs to be delivered by the sheriff. We make arrangements for him to drop it off on his way home from work.

We end the call, and I walk over to the patio. As I stare out, my mind is reeling ninety miles an hour. I've gotten myself into some pretty crazy situations before, but being alone right now in my wife's apartment—without her, without any electricity and without knowing what tomorrow holds—is about the most absurd thing I can think of. My life...it's...it's a train wreck.

Knock, knock.

Has it been an hour already?

I look through the peephole and sure enough, it's him. Sheriff Jones. I slowly open the door, trying to not to appear nervous.

"Brian Collins?" he asks.

"Yes, sir. That's me."

"I need you to sign right here and right here," he directs my attention to his clipboard and hands me his ball-point pen. The lines I need to sign are highlighted so there's no mistaking signing the wrong thing.

"That's it?" I ask and pass the clipboard back to him.

He hands me an envelope, my name clearly written on the outside. "Have a good evening." He turns and walks away, not bothering to answer my question.

Wow, so much for conversation. Well screw him and the broom he flew in on. Personality is definitely not a requirement for his job. Yep, he's just like any other person of authority who wears a uniform—arrogant and stuck on themselves. I slam the door, aggravated by his cockiness.

I turn the envelope over examine it closer. In the upper left hand corner, **Glen and Glen, Attorneys-at-Law**, is pre-printed. Of course, not being from here, the name of the firm doesn't sound familiar. I take a deep breath then rip open the envelope.

I carefully unfold the pages of the documents. My finger rubs across something raised on the back page, no doubt the notary stamp showing the paperwork is indeed legally endorsed. Then, I see it all. In black and white letters, Jennifer Davis Collins, plaintiff vs. Brian Collins, defendant. The paperwork I'm holding is none other than my own divorce papers—Jennifer is seeking a divorce from me. Divorce.

Nooooooo!

The legal terminology doesn't mean much, and I end up scanning the remainder of it. I drop my head down, ashamed. I'm nothing but a total fuckup in life and this is proof.

As I stare at the pages, I wonder what rights I have, if any, with the baby on the way. I don't have money to fight, but surely there's someone out there who can help me—someone who feels sorry for me. Maybe? I reach up to wipe away a lonely tear that's found its way on my cheek.

Why would anyone want to help me? I have nothing. I am nothing. What judge would grant me anything given my history?

I lean back against the wall and slide down to the floor. I feel the tears ready to burst from my eyes. I…I can't. I won't give up. I crumble the divorce papers and throw them across the room. I still love Jennifer. I love her, and I love our baby. I'll…I'll pretend I never got these damn papers, and I'll stay married to her as long as I can. I will win her back.

I stay seated like this for hours, or so it seems. It's now completely dark, both inside and out. Just because I can't see the papers in the middle of the floor doesn't mean they're not there. Something so simple as a few pieces of paper can change so much.

Suddenly, I have an idea. I double check that my keys are in my pocket and feel my way to the door. I don't even bother to lock the door behind me.

****

Not wanting to be seen, I pull into a parking spot at the far edge of the hotel property. The rain has stopped but there's still water standing all across the parking lot. I scan the area looking for one thing—Rebecca's car. On the drive here, I kept going over what I was going to say, how I would approach her. Tonight, baby, she's going to give me some answers—answers that I've waited long enough to find out. I'll get them out of her one way or another.

Instead of waiting for the lobby to clear, I barge right on in the front door. Several individuals are lined up waiting to be checked in. To my surprise though, there's no one at the counter. I look around, but I don't see her. A television plays over in the seating area and I make out the light hum of the ceiling fan overhead. How did I …? Where is…?

Suddenly, a door slams and I see her walk around the corner. Her arms are loaded down with folded bath towels. That is, until she sees me. She stops dead in her tracks and locks her gaze with mine. All the towels she'd been holding fall to the floor.

No one else notices or pays me any attention until I run up to assist her. "Here, let me give you a hand with those."

Her cold-as-ice look penetrates right though me. "What the hell do you want?"

"Rebecca, we need to talk." I try to stay as calm as possible, not wanting to cause a scene with customers in the room. What I'd really like to do though, is get right up in her face and give her a piece of my mind, tell her what I really think of her. But I take the opposite approach, all with a sickly-sweet grin on my face. "Please, I really need to talk to you."

"How many times do I have to tell you, Brian? I don't know where Jennifer is, and even if I did, you'd be the last person I'd tell." Her tone is defensive in nature and filled with anger. There's not a doubt in my mind, she's protecting her friend one hundred percent.

"I thought you knew, Rebecca. Jennifer hasn't called you?" I look her directly in the eyes trying to sound as believable and convincing as possible. "Jennifer came home this morning."

The look on Rebecca's face is priceless. My plan is working beautifully.

"We're going to give our marriage another shot. I can't believe she didn't call you."

"So where is she now?" Rebecca asks, still not so sure I'm telling her the truth.

"She was so exhausted she fell asleep on the couch earlier. She looked sweet, so perfect, lying there. You should see her. Her belly…" I pause for a moment, pretending to get carried away with Jennifer's appearance. "I just need to talk to someone. I need some advice so I don't screw up again."

"Excuse me, but can we just get checked into our room," the gentleman at the front of the line speaks up.

"Oh my God, I'm so sorry," she tells him then precedes to go back behind the counter but not before turning to look back at me. I can tell she's not certain of the bomb I just dropped on her, given the look on her face. The customer hands over his identification just as the phone rings.

"Front desk, this is Rebecca speaking," she says while attempting to type something into the computer at the same time. Instead of waiting at the end of the line, I decide to lean up against the counter, no doubt making her nervous.

"Yes, I have your towels," she snaps. "I'll be right there with them. Give me a few minutes."

She finishes up with one customer and starts to work checking in the next one. She gives me a go-to-hell look and I can't help but smile, upsetting her even more. My standing here is doing a number on her.

"You should see how much Jennifer's belly has grown. She looks unbelievably gorgeous now," I lay it on thick, confusing her even more. "The pregnancy makes her glow."

"Brian, why should I believe you?"

The phone beeps again, and Rebecca snatches the receiver up. I have her right where I want her.

"Yes, I told you I will be right there with your towels. Give me a moment, please." She says to the caller then slams the phone down. "Honestly Brian, I think you're full of shit."

I try not to show any emotion from her remark. That, in itself, should be enough to convince her my story is true. The 'Brian' she thinks she knows would be quick to challenge any negative comment.

"Why would I lie?" I plead my story even more.

"Do you honestly want me to answer that question?"

Okay, bitch, I've had about all I can take. I grit my teeth, fighting hard to stay strong.

The phone beeps yet again. Instead of answering this time, Rebecca picks up the towels, straightening the few that unfolded when they fell to the floor.

"Go take care of your room." I tell her. "I'll be waiting on you right here."

"Alright. I'll be right back." She turns to head out the side door.

Without wasting any time, I step behind the counter and begin pulling out the desk drawers. *It's here somewhere. I have to find it*, I tell myself.

The few remaining customers don't detect any tention between the two of us and obviously don't think it strange for me to walk behind the counter.

Bingo!

I found it. Rebecca's phone is directly on top of her purse. I grab ahold of it and make my way to the door. "Tell her I had an emergency and had to leave." I tell the gentleman who's next in line. He just looks at me, a confused look on his face.

"Brian, what the hell are you doing?" Rebecca's voice startles me.

Before I can make it out the door, I accidently trip over the rug and fall into one of the customers, sending him down to his knees. The phone slides out of my hand and glides a few feet across the floor. Thank goodness it's in one of those shatterproof cases. I scoop it up and run for the front door. Rather than chase after me, Rebecca has no other choice than to tend to the fallen gentleman.

I don't bother to look back but keep charging ahead. I pull my keys from my pocket, jump in my car and speed away.

Chapter 7

Jennifer

I'VE BEEN UNABLE TO FALL asleep tonight, something I should be used to by now. I flip the television from one channel to the next since I can't stand to watch those infocommercials. Unfortunately, that's pretty much all that comes on in the wee morning hours.

I switch the lamp to a brighter setting and pick up the book I'd started reading earlier. I move around trying to get comfortable and put another pillow behind me. I pull the blanket up over my lap even though the temperature inside is relatively mild. It's just one of those habits I have.

Through the curtain I see headlights coming up the driveway. They turn to the left, heading to the main house. I glance down at my phone to see the time—it's one-thirty in the morning. Lately, Todd's been coming home later than usual, hanging out at the library getting in some extra studying before his state test comes up in several weeks. I'd never heard of a library staying open that late but Todd said the twenty-four-hour library was one of the best things he loved about the college he attended. Being able to use it day or night, regardless of the time, had been beneficial to him on many occasions. He said there were numerous students, just like himself, who found it was easier to study late at night and away from home. I guess it made sense, especially for someone who lived in a dorm or had roommates.

I've missed spending time with him since he's back in school again. Todd has a goal for himself and isn't letting anyone or anything get in his way. I've said it before, but I admire him and his dedication to his career. Todd's been true to his word about checking in with me, but his texts or visits aren't as often as I'd like and I still get lonely.

When my parents were here visiting the other day, they couldn't help but like Todd and his parents, Rick and Beth. They felt I was safe and well-taken care of here. The more I think about it, both my parents and Todd's were so much alike in so many ways, it was almost like they'd known each other forever. I hated to see them go, but it wasn't fair for them to have to rearrange their plans. I was just glad they'd managed to squeeze in a few days for me. They promised to be back in a few weeks for a longer stay and to follow up with the lawyer again. By that time, the lease would be up, too, and they'd deal with that as well.

I wait for the headlights to shut off then see the porch light turn off, too. I think about sending him a text, just to say hi, but I know he's got to be exhausted. I glance down at my book trying once again to pick up with the story but it's no use—my concentration is just not here tonight.

Out of the blue, my phone rings and I just about fall off the couch. My heart rate increases, and I need a second to settle down. Being so late, I immediately think of my parents and hope nothing's happened. I'm certain Todd probably noticed the lights on here but he would've sent a text before calling.

I pick up the phone from the side table, surprised to see Rebecca's name lit up. It's been a few days since we last talked and I hope everything is okay. Usually, though, she sends a text first just to see if I'm awake. I shrug off the thought and slide my finger across the screen before it goes to voicemail.

"Hello."

There's nothing but silence on the other end.

"Hello?" I repeat again. "Rebecca, are you okay? Are you there?" I glance down at the phone, afraid I was too late answering, but see it's still lit up.

All of a sudden I hear *click*. She ended the call. Maybe it was a bad connection or she had a customer walk in and she needed to tend to them. Either way, I give her a moment to call back.

Sure enough, my phone starts ringing again.

"Hey Rebecca. Why'd you hang up?"

"It's me, Jennifer. Not Rebecca." I hear the all-too-familiar male voice on the other end and fear immediately sets in.

Brian.

Why the heck is Brian calling me from Rebecca's phone? My hands start to tremble so bad I'm barely able to hang onto it. A sudden ache courses its way through my body and I feel as though I need to throw up. I open my mouth to say something, but I'm in such a state of shock, I can't form any words.

"Jennifer, I know you're there. I know you hear me."

"Noooo. I don't want to talk to you!" I scream loudly.

"Jennifer, please, hear me out," Brian pleads. "We need to talk."

"Why are you calling me from Rebecca's phone? Where is she? What have you done with my friend?" I shout.

I hear him snicker into the phone. *Please, God, tell me that Rebecca didn't give into to his evil ways.* She promised me. She swore on her life, that she'd never tell him where I am.

I take a deep breath and try to regain my composure.

"Why are you calling me from Rebecca's phone?" I ask him again.

"Listen, just hear me out," Brian begs. "Just give me a chance."

"I have nothing to say to you." I realize I don't have to listen to his pleas and demands. There's a simple way to handle all off it. I can hang up. But I know he'll keep calling.

"Please tell me you still love me, Jennifer. Just tell me we can try again. I need you, baby."

"Don't you dare call me baby! I'm done with you. What part do you not get, Brian? We are finished. Over! We are done!" I'm literally screaming now.

"Just tell me where you are. Let me come get you and bring you home. You know you still want me."

When I sat down with the attorney my parents hired to handle the divorce, one of the questions she asked me was if I needed to put a restraining order against Brian—had Brian done any physical harm to me? Was he continuing to threaten me? I explained to her about leaving town in hopes to avoid any confrontation and that I had ended all communication. Had

I made a mistake by not seeking legal protection? Should I have come clean about the bottle he threw at me?

"Brian, I'm going to hang up now. I'm asking you nicely, please don't call me again. I have nothing to say to you. Ever!"

Then it hits me. Brian's outburst can only mean one thing—he got served divorce papers.

"I'll fight you to the end, bitch. Don't think you can get away from me so easily. You may not talk to me now, but you will before this is over. You hear me? It ain't over!"

I pull the phone away from my ear. His words are so loud and brusque. How can someone go from begging for forgiveness one minute, to being rude and hurtful the next?

Click.

I have no choice but to end the call. I will not put myself through anymore of this tonight.

I go to the kitchen and grab a glass of water. Oh, how I wish I could talk to Todd. He'd know the right words to say to comfort me. It was bad enough I was already having trouble falling asleep tonight and now this.

I place my glass in the kitchen sink and turn to walk back to the living room. Out of the corner of my eye, I'm almost certain I see headlights through the front bay windows. Not close to the house but out further near the main road. Surely it's just me just being paranoid. I've considered asking Beth if I could hang some curtains in addition to the mini blinds that are already in place, but now I'm positive—it's something I'm going to take care of first thing in the morning. I realize that curtains and blinds won't do much for protecting me but they sort of give me peace of mind should someone be outside trying to look in.

I run to the front door and double check to make sure it's locked. I also do a quick check of the other windows. Every night it's the same thing—checking locks and blinds—often as many as two or three times. Pathetic, I know.

I sit down on the edge of the couch and tightly grip my phone. Should I call someone just to be on the safe side? But who?

I switch off the TV and the house becomes deadly silent. I don't think I've been this scared since the night I left. All kinds of thoughts run through my mind. Unexpectedly, my phone rings again sending me into panic mode once more. The number looks vaguely familiar but I can't place it. Not wanting to deal with Brian and anymore of his crap, I choose not to answer it—I've already had enough middle-of-the-night phone calls as it is. As soon as my phone screen shuts off, it lights up yet again. Whoever it is isn't giving up. But how do I know it's not Brian?

What I'm curious to know, though, is how did he get Rebecca's phone? I hope nothing's happened to her.

A few seconds after the call, I hear the familiar voicemail alert. Any other time I'd just ignore it, but given tonight's events, I feel I should probably check out the message. If it's Brian's voice then I'll just delete it, but something tells me I need to listen to it.

I give in and dial voicemail.

"Jen, it's me, Rebecca. I need to talk to you. When you get this message, please call me at the hotel. Do not call my cell phone. You

see, Brian took my phone tonight, and I'm afraid he may try to call you. Call me as soon as you get this message."

I let out a big sigh of relief. I'm relieved to know Rebecca stayed true to her word, but this is absurd. I knew Brian was up to no good and that this was just another one of his desperate attempts. It's hard to believe the extreme he'd go to just to talk to me.

Without wasting any more time, I call the hotel.

"Jen, oh my gosh, please tell me that douche bag hasn't tried calling you!" she says before I have a chance to get in a word edgewise.

It's so good to hear my friend's voice. "I was so scared. I thought something had happened to you. Then, I could've sworn I saw lights outside. I thought maybe he'd found me." My words come out so quickly, I find myself gasping for air.

"Slow down, sweetie. It's okay," Rebecca assures me. "That ass hole freaked me out tonight, but he's not going to pull a fast one on me *or* you."

"You think he freaked you out? How do you think I felt hearing his voice?"

"I can only imagine. That's why I wanted to call you as soon as possible to tell you what happened. I need some advice though about what I should do," Rebecca says.

"How did he get your phone?" I ask, not sure if I really want to hear his latest scheme.

"It's the strangest thing. There was this guest who kept calling the front desk requesting extra towels. I politely told the man I'd be there shortly. You know how it gets sometimes between checking in guests and the phone ringing," she tells me. "So, I looked up and there he was. At first he was calm, but then he said he needed to talk to me about you. He claimed you'd come back home to work things out, and he needed advice so he wouldn't screw up again. At first I believed him — he sounded so convincing. But, something told me he was up to no good."

"You've got to be kidding me!" I'm almost in tears, shocked just listening to such a bizarre story. He's...he's got some nerve.

"I just had that feeling he was lying. There's no way you would be back with him without my knowing it. Anyway, the stupid phone rang again and instead of taking the call, I ran out the door to take the towels down to the room. Now that I think about it, I wonder if he set up the whole thing just to distract me. I came back in and found him coming out from behind the desk. He dropped my phone trying to put it in his pocket then tripped over a rug. When he bent to pick it up, a guest got in the way. The guy fell on the floor and I had no choice but to tend to him instead of chasing after Brian."

"Why me, Rebecca? What did I do to deserve this?" I manage to say. After listening to the details, it takes all I've got to fight back the tears. "I don't understand."

"I hate this is so upsetting for you. I'd like to punch him in the face." Rebecca tries to comfort me.

"I know. Me too. Sometimes I just want to give up."

"Don't you dare give up! You are one hundred percent in control of this. You've come too far."

Beep, beep.

I look down at my phone and sure enough, Rebecca's number lights up on the screen.

"He's doing it again," I tell her. "He's calling my phone."

"Just don't look at it. He'll stop eventually."

Beep, beep.

"That's easy for you to say. Maybe it's time I take matters into my own hands. From everything he said to me, I'm pretty certain he got served the divorce papers. So, I think it's time I have his phone turned off."

"I like the way you're thinking. Just the other day I went through and deleted all of our texts. It's like I knew something like this was going to happen."

"You don't know how relieved that makes me feel knowing you covered our tracks. What about Todd's number? Did you have it programmed?"

"I have it saved under the name Uncle John. He'll never figure that one out."

"Well, you know, he *is* crazy. I wouldn't put it past him to call everyone in your contacts." I try to make humor of it all but it's so sad knowing he's capable of doing something that ridiculous. "When it comes to Brian, nothing surprises me anymore."

Beep. Beep.

This time he's calling me from *his* phone. Well, he's about to discover how good a cell phone is with no service. I've had all I can take.

"Here we go again," I tell her. "It's time to put an end to this."

"And as soon as you do, I'll call and have mine turned off, too," Rebecca chuckles. "Talk about being pissed. He's going to be livid. Do you think I need to also call the cops and make a report? Technically, he did steal it."

"You've got a point. There's no way I'm going to be able to sleep tonight, so I'm going to go ahead and contact the phone company. Customer service should be available even this time of the night," I let out a yawn even though I'm not sleepy. "I'll also contact my lawyer first thing in the morning. I'll ask about making that police report and let you know what she says." My nerves have settled some just from talking with Rebecca, but I just want it all to end. I want it to go away for good. Sadly, though, I fear this is only a stepping stone of what's yet to come.

"Promise me you'll try to get some rest. Please?"

"You don't know how much a full eight hours of sleep would mean to me. Thank goodness for naps during the day—it's the only way I'm able to make it," I tell her. "I really wanted to see about finding a part-time job, but with everything going on, maybe it's not such a good idea anymore. Besides, who'd want to hire a big, fat pregnant woman."

"Aww, you're not fat."

"Girl, you wouldn't believe how much weight I've gained. And to know you've not been able to share this pregnancy with me all because of that jerk. It saddens me."

"You've had enough stress these last few months. Give yourself a break and enjoy your time before that precious baby girl gets here. Work can wait." Rebecca can't help but slightly giggle. "I still can't believe I'm going to be an aunt."

"And I can't believe I'm going to be a mom."

When I first took the plunge to leave Brian, it never crossed my mind about being a single parent. I just needed a safe place to keep me and my baby out of harm's way. I wasn't looking ahead to the future—I was only concerned about taking one day at a time. I still don't know where I'll be months from now, but I'm sure liking the feel of it here. It seems like a genuinely nice place to call home.

If my parents weren't traveling now and had a place of their own, I'm pretty sure I would've moved back in with them. But my parents don't need to be hindered because of my… mistakes. They worked hard their whole lives and deserve to enjoy their retirement to the fullest. They are living *their* dream.

Speaking of dreams—it's time I start moving forward. After all, I deserve to have dreams, too.

Without waiting any longer, I make the call to the phone company and have Brian's phone turned off. It's time to have some peace and quiet and a good night's sleep. Within a few minutes, my phone has become silent again and quiet never sounded so good.

Chapter 8

Todd

I FEEL BAD FOR NOT making it home at a decent time this week to check on Jennifer. She assured me she'd let me know if there was anything she needed, but I also know that girl has a lot of pride and doesn't like to ask for anything unless she absolutely has to. She knows I'm just about done with school so even if she did need anything, I don't know if she would even ask. Still, I should've at least made time for a quick visit. It's bound to get lonely.

I noticed when I got home the light was on in the living room. I thought about calling or sending her a text but talked myself out of it since it was so late. I knew it was a possibility she'd just fell asleep, and I would've felt awful waking her up. It's not the first time I've noticed them being on but if I bring it up, would she think I'm checking up on her? She's a grown woman about to become a mother, and she's doesn't need anyone questioning her about something so petty as the lights being left on.

It did occur to me that maybe she needs them on to sleep, that maybe something happened and she's uneasy. Sounds crazy, I know, but after all this time she's still terrified that Brian's going to find her. No one should have to live in fear, and it sucks that there's nothing I can do to convince her otherwise. It's something she's got to work through on her own.

When I finally crawled in the bed, I tossed and turned while thoughts of her occupied my mind—good thoughts mind you. The last time I remember looking over at the clock it was almost three o'clock.

My dad and I have always had a bond between us that most guys my age would envy. He's always complimented me on my decision making skills, and how I've handled myself over the years. Just last week while putting in some hours at the pharmacy, he questioned me again about the possibility of having feelings for Jennifer. He'd asked a while back and I blew him off, but was it that obvious now?

He said he was proud of me for sticking by her and that my good deeds would not go unnoticed. The only thing I could come up with to say was that I was thankful for the way he and my mom had raised me. It was true, but he knew there was something more.

I do believe people are put into our lives for a reason, and I've asked myself many times why my path crossed with hers that day. And though I do consider her a good friend regardless of what happens down the road, I can't lie to myself—I'm falling for her. Maybe when her divorce is finalized, I won't feel so guilty about thinking of her in a romantic kind of way.

"Son, I respect that of you. I really do. But I also know there's a certain sparkle in your eyes anytime her name in mentioned. I realize you're extremely focused on your studies, but don't let a good thing possibly pass you by either." Yeah, my father said that to me.

****

The alarm buzzes, and I roll over to hit the snooze. I'm usually up the first time it goes off, but this morning, I'd give anything to have just thirty more minutes to sleep. I've pretty much trained my body that a few hours rest each night is plenty for me to make it through the day, but this morning I feel like I've had no sleep at all. Images of Jennifer kept running through my mind. What the heck is going on?

The alarm goes off again, and this time I literally crawl out of bed and make my way to the shower. Standing under the steady spray of water, I can't help but think of her even more.

I rinse the shampoo from my hair then grab the washcloth that's draped on the shower bar. As I wipe the soap over my body, I pretend not to notice the erection that I woke up with. I simply can't get her off my mind. How much longer am I going to deny these feelings? The fact that she's technically still married to that scumbag doesn't bother me because I know it's only a matter of time until the divorce is finalized, but what scares the hell out of me is that she may not be ready for another relationship any time soon, and well, no one likes rejection.

I finish with my shower and give myself a onceover in the mirror before getting dressed. It's been so long since I've been involved with anyone sexually, it's no surprise my lingering visitor doesn't want to go away. The last relationship I was in didn't end well because I couldn't separate school and pleasure. I couldn't keep my head where it needed to be so I ended it. I made a promise to myself that my career would come first, regardless of who tried to intervene in my life.

This situation, though, is different. And with the end of school being so near, should I risk it? Should I pursue something just to see where it goes?

I throw on a polo shirt and khaki shorts and head downstairs to see what Mom's fixed for breakfast. My mom is sort of old-fashioned in that she still likes to fix a hearty meal for my dad and me every morning. Don't get me wrong, I enjoy it since sometimes I don't get much of a break during the day, but she's spoiled me over the years. Just as I reach the bottom of the stairs I notice a familiar voice coming from the kitchen — Jennifer. Seems mom has invited her over to eat, too.

It doesn't take long for my hard-on to return. Just seeing her and knowing I'd been dreaming of her causes my cheeks to redden. I pray she doesn't notice the bulge in my shorts.

"Morning," she says.

I detect something is off just from the tone of her voice. For the most part she's always cheerful and friendly, but today she sounds different. Maybe she's tired and didn't sleep well or maybe she's just not a morning person. I hope that the light being on last night doesn't have anything to do with it.

"Morning." I reply, not only trying to hide the shock of seeing her here but not wanting to draw any attention to 'my issue.' I try to tug at the bottom of my shirt without being too obvious.

I walk over to the refrigerator and pull out the milk. I'm careful not to laugh out loud at myself when I notice both of my hands trembling while pouring the milk into a glass. *Dude, you need to get ahold of yourself.* I don't think I was this nervous the first time I kissed a girl. I carefully return the jug back to the refrigerator then walk over to the table to take a seat.

I see Jennifer's glass is almost empty and feel bad for not asking if she'd like a refill.

"So what brings you by this morning?" I ask, hoping the coloring in my cheeks has returned to normal. I'm happy—actually more than happy—to see her but the look she's wearing tells me something's up.

"I was sitting out on the porch this morning when your mom walked out to get the newspaper. She invited me over, figured I could use some company."

That's my mom—always looking out for everyone.

"So, have you been doing okay? I've been meaning to stop by, but I've been so overwhelmed with one of my classes. I'm counting the weeks 'til I'm finished." I'm really at a loss for words right now, and the only thing I feel comfortable talking about is school. I should be ashamed of myself for not asking about the baby, but I feel so embarrassed sitting here knowing she's the reason for the hard-on I *still* have. Yes, it's still there and causing a little bit of discomfort.

"Physically, I've been doing great," she adds rather quickly then hesitates before saying more. "Brian was just served divorce papers, so I had a little trouble falling asleep last night."

I knew it. I knew there was some reason why she looked so fatigued. "He hasn't tried to contact you has he?" I'm quick to come to her defense, ready to step up and do something to stop him if he has.

"Uhm…kind of." She looks up but doesn't directly look at me while she speaks. "But I took care of it."

"You don't sound so convincing."

"I guess my body is just a little confused. That's all. It's gotten to where all I want to do is sleep during the day and stay awake all night. And his little stunt last night didn't help any, either."

"Oh yeah?" I knew there was more to it; I just needed her to open up. Hopefully, talking about it will help.

"Yeah, well, Rebecca sometimes calls me late at night since she took over the shift I used to have. I didn't think anything about seeing her number show up on my phone. But it wasn't her on the other end of the call." She hesitates before finishing the story. "It was him calling me—Brian took her phone. He…he planned the whole thing, just…so he could talk to me." Her voice quivers and I can see how upsetting it's making her just talking about it. "Something happened at the hotel and Brian managed to get Rebecca's phone from behind the counter. He said things that made me think he'd found me. Not to mention, I thought I saw something outside. I know now it was just my mind playing tricks on me, but I was really spooked given everything that's happened."

"I'm so sorry." I reach over and position my hand on her shoulder. "You know if you ever get scared you can call me. Day or night, it doesn't matter, and I don't mind coming down to the house to sit with you. Even if you need me to stay long enough for you to fall asleep. You need your rest and you surely don't need to be getting upset. It's not good for you or the baby." If she'd only let me know what she was going through, I'd have been there in a moment's notice.

"Thanks, but I didn't want to bother you. I know you've got your own life to live rather than being bothered by me and my problems." She drops her head down again.

"I'm serious. Call me next time. I mean it. Sometimes I'm still wired from studying so much that it's hard for me to fall asleep as well." I hope I sound convincing enough to her.

Mom walks back into the kitchen—neither of us even aware that she'd left to give us some privacy. A few moments later my dad joins us. The conversation shifts to the pharmacy since they'll both be leaving right after breakfast. Just because the subject was changed doesn't mean I'm through discussing what happened with Jennifer—just gives me a reason to talk with her later on.

"You know, if your dad would find a tech to help him open up in the mornings, I'd make sure you all ate like every day." Mom teases as she begins to clear the table.

We all laugh, knowing my mom would do anything to get out of helping dad out with the family's business. Don't get me wrong, she enjoys being there and especially because it allows them to spend the day together, but she also misses out on so much around here.

Dad doesn't waste any time adding to what mom said. At first, I think he's only teasing, but the more he says, I realize just how serious he is.

"I'm trying to talk Jennifer into helping out—you know, by taking your mom's place. I told her how you started out being a tech before deciding to enter pharmacy school. With the accelerated classes at the Community College in town, she could be a certified Pharmacy Technician in no time." Although dad is speaking to me, I know he's wanting me to contribute my say on the subject. Seems he's not the only one who's grown fond of Jennifer, either.

"Maybe after the baby is born," Jennifer speaks up. "It does actually sound like something I'd be interested in. But then there's the baby to think about, too. I'm not sure how I would feel putting her in a daycare with her being so young."

It's a sensitive matter that Jennifer might find upsetting—what mother wants to put her baby into daycare right after they're born? I hope she doesn't get the wrong idea that my parents want her to do something in exchange for staying here.

"Well, I hate to crash this party, but I need to be on my way to class." I stand and push my chair underneath the table. I figured Jennifer might do so, too, but she actually seems content talking with my dad more about the job offer. I'm not done discussing the matter about Brian and his latest stunt, but it'll give me a reason to visit with her later on.

I leave the three of them sitting at the table and grab my keys off the counter. I toss my backpack over my shoulder then walk over to give mom a kiss on the cheek. I really can't handle hearing my dad talking to Jennifer about a job. If she were my wife, I'd do everything I could to make sure she got to stay at home with our baby for as long as she wanted. But, that's the thing. She's not my wife or even my girlfriend—yet. In time, once she gets everything situated and this jerk is finally gone from her life for good, I might just ask her out. It's no secret the effect she already has on me.

I arrive at school with plenty of time to spare before my first class. I pull out my laptop to check over a few of my notes then start getting everything ready for my lab work. The instructor is running behind this morning so I click off of my notes and check my email. There are a couple of messages pertaining to graduation and reminders of important dates, but other than that, it's mostly advertisements and spam. Before closing out my email, I notice an ad for Flowers.com in the side margin. Would it be inappropriate to send Jennifer flowers?

Just something simple to brighten her day. Before I can talk myself out of it, I click on the link and start the ordering process.

Since roses are more about love and romance, I look for something that's more fitting for friendship. Lord knows I don't want to send her something that will push her away or scare her. The last thing I want to do is pressure her. I'm not that kind of guy and I think she realizes that just from the conversations we've shared.

I finally settle for an arrangement of sunflowers. If you've ever seen a field of them before, then you know just how stunning and breathtaking they are. Their beauty is spectacular. I hold my breath then hit the order button, hoping I'm not making a mistake.

Chapter 9

Brian

I WAKE UP AND RUB the knot that's formed on the back of my neck. I have no idea what time it is, but I know I was awake a good bit of the night. I look around the apartment and see the sun shining through the patio blinds and assume it must be mid-morning.

For just one small moment, while talking to Jennifer on the phone last night, I had hope that there was still a chance for us. As the conversation continued—and had progressively gotten uglier—I think I only pushed her further away. I said some pretty horrible things just before she hung up on me, and, well, it's too late to take them back now.

I still can't believe I was managed to get Rebecca's phone from the hotel. That was pretty slick on my part. I just knew she was going to show up here, banging on the door and causing a scene, but she didn't. Surprisingly, she never tried calling either. The way I feel towards her, though, if she'd shown up, I probably would've smashed the phone against the wall right in front of her. I despise her *that* much.

I kept calling Jennifer from both phones, praying she'd give in and eventually come to her senses. God, she's got to know she still needs me just like I still need her. The only thing I managed to accomplish was draining the batteries down to almost nothing. Eventually, I nodded off.

Speaking of phones, I look over at the coffee table and see them both in the same spot I left them in. I grab the one in the pink case and swipe my finger across the screen. Just maybe there's enough charge left so I can send Jennifer one more text.

Something about the screen looks different, but I'm not sure exactly what it is. I look in the right hand corner to check the signal strength since sometimes reception can be limited here, but no bars are lit up. In fact, the symbol that shows phone service doesn't show either. I sit up, hoping that'll fix it. Still, nothing changes on the screen. The yellow 'low-battery' alert is lit up, but I go ahead and restart it, hoping it'll clear up whatever's going on.

Once the screen restores itself and the rebooting process is finished, I tap the phone symbol. Jennifer's number and all the times I called light up on the screen. I scroll through the list, almost embarrassed that I made so many attempts to talk to her. Hell, I'm not sure I would've answered either.

I get up and walk over to the door. Just maybe she's had time to think about things and she'll answer. I press the call button and wait for it to start ringing.

A pre-recorded message comes on announcing the phone is no longer in service. "Shit!" I say out loud. It only means one thing—Rebecca had her phone shut off. I guess I can't blame her but that would also explain why she never bothered to call from the hotel line or show up here trying to get it back. She took the easier approach. I thought for sure she'd have put up more of a fight to get her phone back.

It may not work anymore as far as service goes, but it still shows all the previous phone activity, including phone calls and texts. If something looks out of the ordinary or maybe linked to Jennifer, I can always check the numbers from my phone.

I scroll through countess numbers, most of them being ones already programmed in with a name. When Jennifer's name doesn't appear at all, I back out and look through the list of contacts. Sure enough, Jennifer's name and number is there but there's no activity to show with it. Maybe I was wrong and the two of them haven't been in touch. My gut tells me that's not the case though.

Next, I go through the text messages. One by one, I read them and but find nothing involving Jennifer. Even the texts between Rebecca and her fiancé don't mention anything pertaining to either of us. There are other texts between people I don't know, apparently family members of Rebecca's or people she goes to school with, but that's it. I come up empty-handed again.

Next, I look through the pictures that are saved on the phone. It's frustrating to scroll through them and see the ones of Jennifer and Rebecca together, out having a good time. None of them look recent from what I can tell. I'd give anything to be able to see that smile on Jennifer's face again, just like the one in some of these pictures. She had such an outgoing personality and she loved life—until I showed up and changed everything.

It's too painful looking through all these photos—the girl I love is gone and I'm doing everything I know to do to get her back. I go back over to the coffee table and grab my own phone. If I can just get her to listen to me.

"What the hell?" I say once the screen it lit up. Something's not right with my phone, either.

I tap a couple of the keys and nothing. It's as though the phone is basically frozen. I grab the charger off the table and walk outside. It sucks having to come out here just to charge my damn phone. I give it a few seconds for the light to show it's charging, then I restart it.

No! God-damn it! Don't tell me my phone has been deactivated, too. The charger prevents me from walking very far, but the same "not active" symbol is in the upper right hand corner of the screen. *Fuck! Fuck my life! This is my god-damned phone!*

One thing is clearly evident—both Jennifer and Rebecca are in on this together. They did this so I wouldn't be able to contact either of them. I feel the anger building inside me, and I fight hard to control it. I snatch the charger from the wall and head back inside the apartment. I pick up Rebecca's pink phone and, with as much force as possible, I throw it across the room. It hits the side of the refrigerator and falls in the floor, scattering into many pieces. Without thinking, I do the same thing to my phone. Instead of hitting the refrigerator, though, the phone hits the wall behind the kitchen sink, knocking over the dish detergent and a bottle of hand soap. The noise is loud, but I don't care anymore. I don't fucking care! If the neighbors upstairs or the people across the hallway hear it, I don't give a fuck! I'm sick of this game *both* of them are playing. That's right, both of them. I knew there was more to it than either of them were letting on. They…they were trying to play me for a fool.

Right now, I'm livid. The more I think about them pulling a fast one over on me, the angrier I get. I grab the pillows from the couch and hurl them across the room. I snatch the lamp off the side table and heave it towards the television.

The CD's and videos underneath the TV stand scatter across the floor. Not caring that my actions are similar to those of a spoiled-brat kid throwing a temper tantrum, I jump up and down on top of them. *Snap. Crunch. Crack.* The floor is a littered mess. I'm having myself a good time, down to the point I even pick up the TV and smash it to the floor, too. There's no electricity so what's the point? It's not like I can watch it. Stupid bitch should've taken it all with her.

As if I can't do anything worse, I pick up the coffee table and chunk it towards the patio. The glass doors shatter into a million pieces and the blinds swirl around in the breeze. *What the fuck did I just do?* There's not a doubt in my mind now that someone had to have heard the racket.

I move on to the kitchen. I open the cabinet doors and sweep everything out. Pots and pans, glasses, cups, plates, silverware—you name it—everything is in the middle of the floor. No one is going to pull a fast one over on me and get by with it. I take in a deep breath while scanning the room—yep, looks like a tornado touched down.

And then, just for the finishing touch, I grab hold of the microwave, and with as much force as I can, I throw it towards the hallway. With a loud bang, it hits the door, putting a big gash in it before landing in the floor. The microwave door pops open and the glass turntable slides halfway out.

I go to the bedroom and grab my duffel back from the closet. Uncertain what's really clean or dirty anymore, I start tossing clothes inside. I cram as many things inside the bag as I possibly can and force the zipper to close. I don't even bother to change out of the clothes I still have on from yesterday—it's not like I've done anything to get them dirty. I look around the room one last time just to make sure I'm not leaving behind anything of importance.

My gaze lands on Jennifer's jewelry box. I slide open the drawers and examine the contents. Most of it appears cheap and not of any substantial worth. Even a pawn shop wouldn't consider the stuff worth anything. Maybe I couple dollars, at the most. Then, I see it—the bracelet I gave her for Christmas. I hold it in my hands while I contemplate whether or not to take it. *I gave this to her. I gave this fucking bracelet to her.*

Tears work their way into my eyes. *Don't do this, Brian. Don't let that fucking bitch get to you.*

It's not like she's coming back here. I stuff it, along with as much of the other jewelry as I can possibly fit, into my pockets.

I rip the sheets from the bed and stand the mattress up on its end. I don't think I've bothered to make it up since she left. What's the use anyway? I've been sleeping on the couch most of the time and trying to stay cool. I pity whoever has to clean up this mess because it sure isn't going to be me. Yeah, I'd say I did a pretty good job tearing up the place.

I grab my bag and head for the front door. I hear noises coming from the apartment overhead but the cops would've been here by now if they'd suspected something down below. Just goes to show how little people pay attention to things anymore—even when it's furniture being flung across a room.

I don't bother closing the door behind me. What's the use?

I stand on the edge of the sidewalk and look around, figuring this is the last time I'll see this place. It's...it's all about to be a part of the past. The early morning sun is blinding, and I bring my arm up to shield it from my eyes. Yep, this is goodbye.

I toss everything in the backseat and back out. Just a few more minutes before I'm done with this damn town. It's brought me nothing but grief and heartache. I stop for traffic at the end of the exit, uncertain as to which way to go. Left or right? It doesn't make much difference to me.

Just as I get ready to pull out, two cop cars come from around the corner, and I have to hit my breaks to keep from getting hit. *Fuck!* I watch them pull into the apartment complex, their sirens silent but their lights flashing in all different directions. My gut tells me they're here for me and I know I've left just in the nick of time. I turn to the right just as two more cop cars come flying into view.

I accelerate quickly knowing time is valuable. I look down at the gas gauge and see I've got less than a quarter of a tank remaining. It's not much, but if I can make it to the next town, I'll have a better idea of where I'm going.

I can't stand living like this, never having a set goal or plan in place. It's time I started doing something right for a change and not constantly fucking up.

I merge into the traffic on the interstate and blend in with the other drivers. The sign on the side of the road indicates the next exit is twenty miles ahead. If I can find a pawn shop there, I can get rid of some of this fake jewelry. It's too bad I ruined the TV and all those CDs and videos. I probably could've gotten a couple bucks for them, too. If nothing else, maybe an individual would've been willing to take them in exchange for some cash or even a tank of gas. I should've thought about that before I showed my ass and acted like an idiot.

Chapter 10
Jennifer

I SPENT A GOOD PART of the morning having some much needed girl talk with Todd's mom, Beth. Even though she's close in age to my own mother, I can't tell you how good it felt just to have some adult interaction.

We talked about so much: the baby and the changes my body has gone through since becoming pregnant; the classes I'd been taking when I was still in school and what my plans had been; my parents and the jobs they'd had prior to retiring; and what I wanted for my future now that everything in my life had taken a detour. The one subject we didn't discuss, though, was Todd. It was like spending time with Rebecca except Beth's older. I was amazed just listening to her.

Beth brought up when she was pregnant—all those years ago, she reminded me—and how having a baby impacted her marriage to Rick. It hadn't been easy for either of them, but she wouldn't have traded it for anything. They'd both had their ups and downs, but had been there for each other during both the good and bad times.

As embarrassing as it was, I went into more detail about Brian and how we'd met. What the hell had I been thinking when I offered to let him move in? Beth had no idea I'd went through so much. She said it was no wonder I looked tired all the time. Then, I mentioned last night and the latest stunt he'd tried to pull stealing Rebecca's phone. She assured me—just as Todd did—that anytime I got scared I was more than welcome to come up to the main house. If was a big relief getting it all out in the open.

By mid-morning I figured I should be getting back down to the guest house. Beth had things she needed to do as well as make her appearance at the pharmacy. We said our goodbyes and she made me feel so much better when she gave me a hug.

Just after two o'clock in the evening, a knock on the door startles me awake. The last thing I remember was reading on my kindle. I slowly make my way to the door and look out from behind the curtain before opening it. An older lady is standing at the edge of the porch holding an arrangement of flowers. My first instinct is they must be for Beth and she's at the wrong house. Since Beth left earlier and won't be home until later, I figure I might as well take them from the delivery driver just so they don't have to come back later on.

"Can I help you?" I ask while I carefully open the door.

"Yes, I have a delivery for Jennifer Collins," she says with a smile on her face. "Are you Jennifer?"

"Yes ma'am," I politely tell her, "but I'm not expecting any flowers."

"Honey, that's what most people say. I just need you to sign my clipboard and I'll be on my way." She passes it over to me and I reach for the pen that's attached by a ribbon.

I'm still not certain I heard her correctly. She said they're for me? Not Beth? What if...oh no, please don't let this be another one of Brian's ploys.

I sign my name and she hands the flowers over. The vase is filled with a beautiful arrangement of sunflowers—so breathtakingly beautiful, I can't take my eyes off of them. I set them down on the kitchen table and blankly stare at the attached card. Should I? Do I really have to know who they're from?

Curiosity gets the best of me, so I pull the envelope from the plastic stick and slide my finger under the sealed flap. Holding my breath, I slowly pull out the card.

"I thought you might need a little something to brighten your day. Thinking of you. Todd"

I reread the card several more times before placing it down on the table next to the arrangement. This is a nice surprise for sure. I never would've expected them to be from him.

I find my phone and sit down at the table. I know the proper thing to do would be to call and thank him, but the thought of doing so sends butterflies through my stomach. If I'm getting all jittery about flowers from him, I could only imagine how I'd feel if he'd ran his finger down my cheek, if he leaned over to whisper something in my ear, if he... Oh dear. Is it possible? Have I really started falling for him?

I decide to send him a text instead.

Me: Not sure the occasion, but the flowers are beautiful. Thank you for thinking of me.

Almost instantly, he sends a message back.

Todd: Just thought you deserved a little something for the special person that you are.

Me: Aww. Thank you again. That's so sweet of you to say.

Todd: Would you like to have dinner with me tonight?

I drop the phone down on the table after reading his last message. Did he just really ask me to dinner?

Me: Seriously?

Todd: Yes. Seriously. I feel as though I've neglected you lately. How does 7 o'clock sound?

Me: Okay, I guess.

Todd: See you then.

Me: ☺

As I place the phone down on the table I notice my hands are trembling. I admit, I desperately need to get out of here for a little while because I'm going crazy staying in every single day. Other than my trips to the doctor, the grocery store and the library, I never go anywhere. Besides, this is just a friendly outing. Right? Todd knows how I feel about dating and relationships so I don't know why I'm getting so worked up about it.

I go back and reread his texts again just to make sure I read them correctly. Oh, Lord could this be a ...date?

I decide to do something special for myself, something I've not done in a very long time. It's time I get out of here.

I slip on a pair of sandals and grab my purse and keys. Just last week after leaving Dr. Crane's office, I saw a sign for a nail salon. Since my belly has gotten so big, I've sort of let my toe nails go. This is the perfect opportunity for a pedicure. The only thing missing is Rebecca. We always got our nails done together—there was even a time we splurged on a massage. Those were the days.

I make the short drive into town and find the nail salon with no problem. I pull into the closest parking spot I can find to the entrance then glance around before getting out of my car. I hope that one day I'll be able to go places without living in fear of Brian seeing me. I know it's only been a short time since I left—merely a few weeks—but it's eventually got to get better. I can't live like this forever.

Apparently I've come to the salon at a good time because the ladies don't seem to mind doing a little extra. Not only do they talk me into a manicure, but I get to spend additional time in the massage chair. It's so relaxing and just what I need.

When I'm finished, there's still about an hour or so before I need to head back. So, I walk down the side of the street checking out all the little boutiques and gift shops. I'm amazed at all these cute stores. A little further down I see the sign for the **Williams Family Pharmacy**. I consider stopping in but talk myself out of it. What if Todd's there putting in a few hours before he heads home for…our date. Just thinking about it makes me nervous all over again.

Instead, I walk inside **The Baby Buggy**, a cute specialty shop for infants and children. The fact that I'm so close to having a baby of my own still blows my mind. I've bought just a few things for her but there's still so much I need to get before she arrives. The last time I spoke to my mom she told me she had started buying baby things, and she couldn't wait to share all of them with me. Even so, I know I'll never be completely ready for a newborn.

I glance around the little shop and I'm amazed at all the cute things. Some items appear homemade with their smocking and stitching. I want to buy one of everything, but I know that's not feasible. I remind myself she'll be just fine wearing normal baby clothes instead of these elegant, dainty dresses. Still, it doesn't hurt to look.

One little pink dress catches my eye. It's a simple cotton design with ducks stitched around the collar. The dress is fancier than anything I'll probably ever need, but there's something about it that causes my heart to flutter.

Speaking of fluttering, the baby has been very active the last few days. Once I got used to her movements, it was the neatest thing to watch the little bumps that formed on top of my belly. Seeing them move from side to side was amazing. My only regret was not having someone to share this joyous occasion with.

I realize this is the only way it can be for now. Brian was a mistake, a part of my life I can't change. And, because of his actions, I'm missing out on many other things, too. None of my friends from high school or co-workers will get to throw me baby showers. Everything—I'm having to do alone. All because of him.

I glance down at my watch and realize I've spent way too much time here. I grab the pink dress and pay for it before I can talk myself out of it.

Back out at the car, I can't help but look at the pharmacy one more time before driving away. I admire the Williams family, more than they'll ever know. Such kind and generous people. I guess I shouldn't be too surprised Todd inherited it from them, too.

On the drive back, I think about my divorce and how it will actually feel to be single again. If you'd have told me a year ago I'd be in this predicament, I'd never in my wildest imagination believed you. Yeah, who prepares for this kind of stuff? And me, of all people for it to happen to.

My attorney assured me it'd eventually all work out, but I should expect a few bumps in the road. I guess Brian taking Rebecca's phone was one of those bumps. I'm still keeping my fingers crossed that Brian will just sign the papers and we can put this marriage behind us. I'm confident that I can raise this child just fine without him. I'd hate for any of his bad habits to negatively affect me or the baby.

I have no plans to put his name on the baby's birth certificate. Call me cruel or whatever, but that's just the way I want it to be. I'm willing to sacrifice any and all future support he may try to offer. He has shown me more than once how little he cares about me. And, if he can't care for me, he surely can't care for a baby, too. He's done nothing to earn the right to be called a father. I know my baby didn't ask for any of this, but once she's older, I'll explain to her why things turned out the way that they did.

Besides, being a single parent right now doesn't mean it'll always be that way. I'm sure I'll date again and eventually find the right man that'll accept my baby as his own.

I get back home and run upstairs to pick out something to wear tonight. My selection is very limited with the few clothes I have, but that's okay. I didn't believe in spending a whole lot of money on maternity clothes since I'm only wearing them for a few months anyways. I'm okay with mixing and matching the ones I do have, and knowing Todd the way that I do, he'll be perfectly content with whatever I'm wearing. The good thing about leggings, they can be made to compliment any outfit.

After showering, I fill the tub with water, adding in some scented bath salt. It's not easy climbing in and out of the tub anymore but a relaxing warm soak is just what I need to settle my nerves—good nerves, mind you.

When I'm done, I go ahead and get dressed. As I'm standing in the mirror looking at my reflection, I can't help but feel like something's missing. Jewelry—a nice necklace is just what I need to compliment my outfit. I regret not bringing more of my jewelry along with me, but because I left so suddenly, I primarily wasn't concerned with jewelry. I left some really nice pieces behind that I'm sure I'll never see again. I thought about having Rebecca stop by the apartment one day when Brian wasn't there, but now that things have progressed and gotten too out of control, I'd never consider putting her at risk. Jewelry can be replaced but a life can't.

With the lease being up, it's just a matter of time until he's gone. And, since the divorce papers have been served, the leasing office should be notified within a couple days that's it's okay to begin the eviction process. Talk about getting a slap to the face—Brian won't know what hit him. I can just see his face when he puts his key in the lock and it no longer works. He's going to be pissed. I just hope the management staff has back-up because with his temper, they're going to need it.

I'm thankful I won't have to be there to see it take place. Now the divorce papers, well, that's another story altogether.

I put the finishing touches on my hair and take one last look in the mirror. Turning to the side, I pull my top tight around my belly. Yep, there's a baby growing inside me and she's getting bigger every day.

I double check my phone for the time Todd's supposed to arrive even though I already know he's supposed to be here at seven. I'm nervous, okay? I make my way into the kitchen and stare at the vase of sunflowers again. Wow, Todd is definitely gaining credibility. I mean, I knew he was an incredible guy, but the flowers, they were just what I needed. If I hadn't met him and his grandfather on that horrible day…well, I don't know what would've happened. So much changed from that day on.

My phone rings and panic sets in—Brian, or even worse, that Todd's had to cancel our date. I force myself to look at the screen. Relief washes over me when I see it's my dad.

"Hey, dad. I wasn't expecting to hear from you," I say almost too cheerily into the phone. I'm not quite ready to tell either of my parents about my plans for tonight. "Is everything okay?"

"Hey, baby. Your mom and I are just fine," he replies even though I sense something is wrong. "And what about you? How are you feeling?"

"I'm okay. Why does your voice sound a little strained?" I call him out on it because I'm not dumb—I know when's something's not right.

"Jenn…." My dad hesitates for a moment and a cold chill works its way through my body. I knew it—something's happened. "There was a situation today…and your mother and I feel it's best that you know about it."

I sit down on the couch, suddenly feeling light-headed.

"Jennifer…" he begins.

I cut him off. "Dad, what's wrong? What's going on?"

"Look, baby. Settle down," He tries to reassure me, but it's too late. The tears are waiting to spill from my eyes. I already know it's not going to be good. "A lady from the apartment complex called me earlier this evening. A situation occurred at the apartment, and I feel you need to know. I've already spoken with the authorities and your attorney about it."

"Authorities? My attorney?" I ask, not liking where this is headed.

"It's okay, for now. Just calm down."

That's easy for him to say. I'm the one who's had their world turned upside down. What more could possibly be wrong now?

"Dad, tell me. I need to know."

"Shh, settle down. Apparently, the neighbors who lived above your unit heard a commotion going on downstairs and felt they needed to call the cops. Said something didn't seem right from all the noises they'd heard. When the cops arrived, they found the apartment was…it was trashed, honey."

"Oh no." Barely able to speak, my voice trembles and I do everything I can to hold myself together. "And they feel Brian was responsible?"

"Brian was nowhere to be found, but the cops feel he hadn't long been gone long. They questioned a few people and said they saw his car leaving right before the authorities showed up."

"Oh my God!"

"That's not all," he continues. "Apparently, the electricity's been shut off, and Brian was using candles just to see his way around. They found a couple of cell phone parts scattered throughout the kitchen, too. The furniture was in disarray and all the cabinets and drawers were emptied out onto the floor. A few holes were noticed in the walls as well. Something obviously set Brian off and this was his way of getting even. I'm so sorry to have to tell you this over the phone."

I'm speechless. Although this shouldn't surprise me at all given Brian's behavior, I never expected this to happen. It's a shame he's so messed up that he felt the need to resort to this behavior.

"Baby, you're not saying anything." My dad's voice is full of concern.

"I...I don't know what to say, dad."

I hear something on the porch and I suddenly remember Todd—he was supposed to be here any minute. Sure enough, he's standing just outside the front door, ready to knock. Seeing my smeared makeup and swollen eyes, he grabs ahold of my hand and walks me over to the couch.

I finish speaking with my dad then place my phone down on the coffee table. I try to hold myself together but one look at him and I completely lose it. I feel like everything is falling apart. Todd pulls me to him and wraps both arms around me. It's exactly what I need.

He whispers softly, "It's all going to be okay. Trust me."

Chapter 11
Todd

WITHOUT KNOWING WHAT'S GOING ON, it's kind of hard for me to say the right words to her. I just know that she's upset, and I don't like seeing her this way.

After a few moments, she pulls away and I hand her another tissue. This helpless look on her face…it's killing me. "Is there something I can do?"

I give her a moment to compose herself, then reach up to push a strand of her hair behind her ear. Without thinking, I caress the side of her cheek with my finger. Once I realize what I'm doing, I snatch my hand back before she chastises me. The last thing I want to do is cross the line where she's concerned.

"Why does my life have to be so complicated?" she asks. "Where did I go wrong to have such horrible things happen?"

"What's going on, baby." I can't help it and place the palm of my hand against her cheek. I turn her face just slightly so that she sees the concern in my eyes. I'm here for her, whatever she needs.

Slowly, she begins to open up. As she rehashes everything her father told her about Brian, I'm at a loss for words and have trouble comprehending that someone could be so cruel and destructive and so… heartless. The worst part, I'm still struggling to figure out how she got mixed up with him in the first place.

"I'm so sorry, Todd," she adds. "I know we had plans to have dinner tonight but do you think we can do this another time? I just don't think I'm up for eating anything right now."

As hard as it was for me to send her the text asking her to dinner, I completely understand. I'd never pressure her under any circumstances. "I tell you what, why don't I just order us a pizza? We don't have to eat it right now, but you might get hungry later on."

"You know, you're something else," she says and reaches over to hug me. "Thank you."

While I order the pizza, Jennifer goes to the bathroom to wash her face. When she returns, I notice she's changed from the cute top she had on earlier and into a t-shirt. No doubt, something she's more comfortable in. I regret not telling her how nice she looked, though. She'd obviously put a lot of time into getting ready since I'd never seen her hair curled before.

We make small talk, almost like we're both too shy to say anything. I know that's not the case, but at least I feel she's got a better grip on things now. When I first got here, I didn't know what the hell had happened.

I bring up my schooling, something I'm always comfortable talking about. I pushed myself so hard the first few weeks trying to get ahead, I almost don't know what to do with myself now. I'm actually going to have some free time coming up.

"I can't tell you how much I admire you. You...you're such an inspiration," she says. I can tell, just from the way she looks at me, that she truly means it.

It's been rough, and there were many times I thought I'd never make it. But I trudged on. At night, I'd see my father and see how proud I'd made him. We'd discuss problems I was having in certain classes, and he'd offer me advice. After all, he'd been down the same path, too.

Not wanting to spend the entire evening talking about me, I shift the subject to Jennifer and what she'd like to do once she's finished with school. I avoid mentioning 'if' she goes back and try to focus more on 'when' she goes." I don't want her to ever look back on her life with regrets.

"I'm so close to graduating, I'd be crazy not to finish," she states.

We're interrupted by a knock at the door. I pull out my wallet to take care of the food and tip. When I walk back into the kitchen, I see she's pulled out some plates for us to use.

"Change your mind about eating?" I ask and set the box on the counter.

"Well, I am eating for two, you know," she laughs and I'm so happy to see a smile return to her face again.

"Thanks for letting me stay and order this for us," I nod towards the food and pull out another slice. "I just couldn't let you be here alone, especially after you told me what had happened."

The room falls silent again, neither of us knowing what to say next. Just when I stand up to take our dirty plates and the pizza box to the kitchen, Jennifer attempts to get up, too.

"Ohh," she cries out and clutches the bottom of her stomach. Her face is pained and it's evident something's not right.

"Are you okay?" I ask her, quickly setting everything back down and placing my hand on her shoulder.

"I'm not sure. I just had a really sharp pain, but it's easing up. I probably just stood up too soon." The coloring has drained from her face and I'm not really convinced that she's fine.

"Why don't you sit back down for a minute. Maybe it'll ease off."

She slowly sits down on the couch while keeping her hands positioned underneath her. "That's better," she says.

I get rid of everything and hurry back to the living room. I notice she's propped her feet up on the table but nothing about her expression has changed—she still looks as though something's wrong. I turn on the TV and hand her the remote to scroll through the channels.

"Why don't you find us something to watch? If it's okay with you, I'll stick around for a little bit until you think you're okay."

"Aww, thank you. It was the weirdest feeling."

I take the seat beside her, doing everything within me not to reach over and hold her hand.

Confession time here. Every time she tells me of something horrible that's happened, I just want to beat the shit out of whoever is responsible. I'm so tired of her getting hurt. Life's not dealing her a fair set of cards. I'm falling for her and there's nothing I can do to stop it. There, I've finally admitted it.

It's getting harder and harder to be near her without trying something. If I'd met her first, that could be my baby she's carrying, and I promise you, I'd be treating her a hell of a lot better than that idiot. I'd never put her through the hell that he has.

"Can I get you something to drink? Maybe a glass of water?" I ask, willing to get her anything she needs.

"No, no thanks. I think whatever it was has passed now." She looks over at me and I literally have to keep myself from leaning forward and kissing her. Her breath is warm against my face—we're sitting just that close to one another.

"You know I'd do anything for you." I say the words without realizing it.

"Todd…"

"I'm sorry. I wasn't trying to force anything on you."

"It's…it's okay."

The room begins to get warm and I feel the sweat form on my brow. She's just so freaking amazing. "How about some fresh air? Maybe you'd like to sit out on the porch?" I suggest when I notice she's stopped scrolling through the channels and left the TV on one of the weather stations.

"That sounds like a good idea. Just let me go to the bathroom first." She stands up and grabs ahold of her stomach again. "I'm okay."

As she heads down the hallway, I notice how slow her steps are. I go ahead and go out on out on the porch, sliding both rockers side by side. Since there's the little gap between the chairs, hopefully it'll keep me from reaching over and taking her hand in mind. It was so tempting just a few minutes ago.

I wonder if Brian regrets anything that he's done to push her away. I just can't imagine how any man would put their pregnant wife or girlfriend in harm's way. Does the fool not realize how good he had it? Just listening to Jennifer tell me what she did for him. Makes me sick thinking about it.

I look down at my watch, realizing she should've already been out by now. I walk back inside and notice the glow of the bathroom light underneath the door. Not wanting to scare her, I call out, "Babe, you okay in there? You're taking a while so I thought I should check on you."

"Todd, something's not right," she calls out from the other side of the door.

"Do I need to come in?" I ask, almost afraid of what I may be walking in on.

"Please," she immediately says, and I open the door without further hesitation. "I don't know what I should do."

I see her sitting on the toilet, and the look on her face says everything—she's scared to death.

"I think my water may have broken. I kept thinking I had to pee and it just wouldn't stop. It's a little bloody-looking, but not bad, though. Do you mind calling your mother ..." She trails off as she clenches her belly again. "I also think these may be contractions instead of stomach pains."

Panic sets in. "Let me grab my phone. Wait. I've got it right here in my pocket," I tell her. I start scrolling through my contacts looking for my mother's phone number when it hits me that I know the number by heart. I feel so stupid. The last thing I want is for Jennifer to start having this baby before we can get her to the hospital.

I tap the symbol to call my mom and listen as it rings a couple of times. "Oh, thank God you answered. Mom, we think I'm in labor. I mean Jennifer. I think Jennifer's in labor," I blab into the phone. I'm so nervous I can hardly believe the words that are coming out of my mouth.

"Calm down, son." My mother says so calmly into the phone. "Your father and I are out at dinner. Is Jennifer near? May I speak with her please?"

I pass the phone to Jennifer who is now taking deep breaths. I run both hands through my hair. *What do I do? Oh, God, what if she's in labor?*

Jennifer hands me the phone back. "Well, what did she say?" I ask.

"You need to grab a blanket or some towels and you need to help me to the car. You can drive can't you?" Jennifer asks.

I can't help but let out a little laugh. "I hope so. What else? Is she coming here? Do we need to meet her somewhere?"

"Todd, calm down. Your mother is in town right now. She and your father are out having dinner. By the time we make it to the hospital, they'll be finished. It'd be senseless for her to drive all the way back out here."

"Yeah, you're probably right."

How can Jennifer remain so calm? She stands up and I turn my head, afraid of what I might see inside the toilet. She grabs ahold of my arm and I admit I shut my eyes. If I look, I...I might get sick...or worse, I might pass out.

"You know I can't let you drive like this?" I manage to tell her.

"Todd, will you please calm down." She can't help but laugh even more. "I'm not driving us anywhere. You are."

I make a quick walk through of the house just to make sure everything is turned off. Then, I grab Jennifer's purse from the bedroom and meet her at the front door.

"Wait right here." I pull the truck up as close as I can to the porch and put it in park. I get out and run around to help her but she's already waiting to get in. Yep, I'd say she's ready to go. Her urgency only adds to my nervousness. I stand behind her as she climbs inside, and I wonder if we shouldn't take her car instead. It'd sure make getting in and out much easier on her. Since time is of the essence, I'll worry about swapping vehicles later.

I take a deep breath and slowly pull away. I'm extra careful not to hit any bumps in the driveway, apologizing to her religiously because my father never bothered to have it paved. She just looks at me and laughs.

Once we're out on the main highway, I switch on my emergency flashers. Even though there's hardly any traffic, I worry we're not going to make it to the hospital in time. It's a little more than ten miles to get there, and, well, you just never know. I concentrate on the road and steal glances her way as often as I can. Surprisingly, she seems calm. Me, on the other hand, that's a different story.

I finally get us there, and I've never been so happy to see a hospital before. I turn into the emergency room entrance and immediately spot my parents standing just outside the doorway. As soon as I stop my truck, dad opens the door and assists Jennifer in climbing out and into a wheelchair. He offers to park the truck for me so I can take her inside. Meanwhile, mom takes Jennifer's bags and walks along beside us.

At the front desk, I explain to the nurse the pain Jennifer started experiencing earlier, and they go ahead and begin the admissions process. I hate leaving her, but the nurse assures me someone will be out shortly to get us.

My mom grabs my hand and walks me to the waiting room. Dad walks in and points out a couple chairs over in the corner. They both detect how nervous I am and dad pats me on the shoulder.

"It's all going to be okay," he assures me.

Easy for him to say—he's not the one having a baby. Well, neither am I, come to think of it.

I can't believe how worked up I am. I'm just thankful I was with her tonight when she started having the pain. Thank goodness she didn't mind my staying after she got that disturbing news from her dad.

Speaking of her dad, I reach inside Jennifer's purse and pull out her phone. I really don't know what to say so I hand the phone to my mom. "Do you mind calling her parents?" I ask. "I'm not sure I'd know what to say."

I stand up and walk to the water fountain. I'm not thirsty, but I take a couple sips anyway. It seems to be taking forever to find out any information on her. As soon as I see the nurse walk into the waiting area, I rush over to her, eager to hear what's going on. She informs us that Jennifer is indeed having contractions. They're carefully monitoring her since there's still a few weeks before she's actually due, but the doctor is on the way to further examine her. We're allowed to visit with her, one at a time, for now, and I immediately stand up and ask for directions.

I knock on the hospital door before slowly pushing it open. I expect to see all sorts of tubes and wires everywhere with things hanging from the ceiling, but that's not what I find at all. I guess what we see on television isn't really true.

Jennifer's sitting up in the hospital, wearing this funky-looking pale green gown. I try not to stare even though there's nothing to really stare at. She almost looks…normal. I lean over to give her a hug and her arms feel heavenly as they wrap around my neck.

"So, how are you feeling?" I ask, uncertain what to really say to her.

"I'm okay. Lots of drugs," she says. "They're keeping a close eye on me but we might be having a baby tonight."

Baby? Tonight?

I inform her that her parents are on their way and that my folks are out in the waiting area. I reach for her hand and tell her I'm proud of her and everything's going to be okay. Then, as if something magical takes over my body, I bring her hand up to my lips and place a gentle kiss on the backside. I believe she senses something as well because the look in her eyes is unlike anything I've ever seen before. A knock on the door separates us and the doctor walks in.

Chapter 12

Brian

IT'S BEEN A COUPLE OF hours now since I left the apartment, and I'm starting to get sleepy. Thanks to another gas container I swiped—yeah, I'm getting to be a pro at it—from the back of a pick-up truck that was left unattended at the rest stop, I manage to drive further than I'd originally expected. People should really pay more attention to the things they leave behind in their vehicles.

Just outside of town, I pull into the first pawn shop I came to. The guy working behind the counter laughs at me when I pull out the jewelry collection I had stuffed in my pocket. I didn't feel it was worth really arguing about with him but I manage to get fifty bucks for it all. He does, though, inquire about the bracelet he'd seen me tuck back into my pocket, and I tell him I'm not ready to part with it yet. He insists on still taking a look at it and offers me an additional seventy-five dollars after he's examined it up close. Maybe he thought it was real. I don't know, but I just can't. I can't let go of it. As bad as I need the money, I reject his offer. After all, it's the one thing that still connects me to Jennifer.

I regret having to show identification just so he can pay me, but I know it's standard procedure for pawn shop transactions now. I've watched the show on TV enough to know how it all works. He doesn't really appear suspicious of anything given that none of the stuff was worth much, but I'm just leery of leaving a trail behind me.

Fifty bucks is more than what I started out with so I should be happy I got that. Another seventy-five would've been nice, though, but I'm not that desperate…yet.

I grab a quick bite to eat and get back on the road again. The further I get down the interstate, the more I feel Jennifer's presence. It's almost as though she's close-by, or that maybe something's happened to her. As hard as I tried to reach out to her, I was stumped. Where had she disappeared to? I didn't have the first lead. The weeks had slowly passed and there wasn't one single sign of her. It was killing me.

I pull off at the next exit, barely able to keep my eyes open. At one time, I'd gotten pretty good at sleeping in parking lots and avoiding the cops so I hope tonight I'll be just as lucky. The exit is dark, and there isn't a gas station or fast-food place in site. So much for the idea of getting some shut-eye.

I drive a little further down the road, not wanting to get too far away from the interstate. With the moon nowhere in the sky, I feel as though I'm the only one for miles around. After several miles, I come up on a building with a flashing sign out by the road. I slow down to check out the place. According to the sign, I'm at **Moe's Bar & Grill**. I pull in and discover hundreds of bikes in the parking lot—interesting, finding a motorcycle club in the middle of nowhere. I weave through the parking lot, working my way towards the back. Music plays from inside the building, and I notice several guys wearing bandanas clustered in groups throughout the lot. Suffice to say, the place is packed.

I pull behind a garbage dumpster, figuring I'll be safe here. I suddenly have the urge to pee so I step out of the car and walk as close to the dumpster as I can while holding my breath. The smell, well, it's not so pleasant. Stale beer and greasy day-old food meet my nostrils. Ugh.

I climb back in the car when I'm finished with my business and crack the car's windows. I'd much rather be hot than smell that stench all night long. It's still relatively early for a Friday night, so I figure I can probably get in a few hours of sleep before everyone starts to leave. I'd be willing to bet these joints don't start closing down until three or four o'clock in the morning.

All of a sudden, I'm awakened at the sound of gunshots being fired, followed by screams.

Bang, bang.

At first, I think I'm dreaming, but after bringing my seat up to the upright position, I realize it's not a dream at all. Men and women wearing leather and boots are running all through the parking lot in search of their bikes. I'm not sure what to make of everything going on. It doesn't take long before I hear the sound of sirens.

Two cop cars, followed by an ambulance, pull into the lot and stop in front of the main entrance. A few minutes later, two more cop cars come barreling in and pull towards the back.

With all of the excitement and hoopla, I know it'll be awhile before things settle back down again. So, I figure it's probably best if I leave and try to find someplace else to get some rest. The last thing I need is to get caught up in the commotion here. I crank my car and ease through the parking lot.

One of the officers notices my car and starts running over towards me. With his hand in the air, he motions for me to stop.

"Going somewhere?" he calls out and steps in front of my car so that I have no choice but to stop.

I roll my window down, ready to admit I have no idea what's going on. "Yeah, I'm just leaving. Didn't want to be in the way of anything." Apparently it wasn't the right thing to say. *Great! Just fucking great!*

"Son, can you pull your car over there please?" he commands and uses his flashlight to point towards an empty spot. "I'd like to take a look inside your car."

"What? What do you mean? Look inside my car? But why?" I mouth off. "I just pulled over to take a leak, man. I don't know nothing about this damn place." I try to persuade the officer but my temper gets the best of me. If there's one thing I don't like, it's confrontation.

"Please pull your car over, sir," he raises his voice, and I realize I'm not going anywhere any time soon. I watch as he says something into the radio that's clipped to his shoulder strap. Unable to make out what he's saying, I start to panic when he walks around behind my car and calls out my license plate number to the person on the other end of the radio.

I do as he instructs and pull into the vacant spot. I'm pissed at myself for picking this damn place to stop—it's just my god-damned luck. How the hell was I supposed to know there was going to be a shooting?

I step out of the car, and the officer immediately instructs me to walk to the back of my car and place my hands on top of the trunk with my legs spread apart. Another officer joins him and while one keeps his gun drawn on me, the other one helps himself to the contents of my car.

I want to say something, but figure it's probably in my best interest if I keep my mouth shut. I don't have anything to hide, and there's nothing in the car, so it's only a matter of time before they cut me loose. Still, I'm pissed it even had to come this far. Just wait, the joke will be on them. They'll see I was telling the truth and that I was only trying to leave. Fuck them!

Per the officer's request, I pull out my wallet and hand over my identification. He stays at his car forever and I can't keep from breaking out in a cold sweat. What if something from my past comes up? I've stayed out of trouble ever since I met Jennifer and surely there's nothing from back home that's still on my record. That kind of stuff comes off after so long, doesn't it? Back then, I just couldn't keep my mouth shut. I always had to have the last say in any situation, and despite my mannerisms—or lack, thereof, it landed my butt in jail a couple times.

I notice a small crowd has gathered around my car, curious as to what is going on with me now, instead of the earlier disturbance that started this whole fiasco. For once, I feel embarrassed.

When it feels like I've been leaning up against my car forever, the officer finally gets out of his car. He walks over to the other officer who's been keeping an eye on me. They talk for a few moments, and, in slow motion, I watch as he reaches behind him and pulls out his handcuffs.

What. The. Fuck. Is. Going. On?

• The dark-haired officer begins to read me my rights while the other one places the handcuffs on my wrists. I go into an instant fog. I don't resist even though I want to fall down on my knees and scream. *"Why me? What have I done this time?"* But I do as they both say and walk with them to the back of one of the patrol cars. I have no fight left in me anymore.

I estimate the ride to the police station to be about fifteen minutes. As they escort me inside, my body is numb. Once the booking process begins, I'm asked by several individuals about who I am, where I'm from, and why I'm here. Nothing makes any sense. I swear, I didn't do anything.

After I verify my residence as that of the apartment complex, the officer asks me why I was so far away from there. Had I not been planning to go home tonight?

How does one answer a question like that? Why is it any of their business if I'm planning to go home or not?

I realize at this moment that this has absolutely nothing to do with the bar brawl. No, the joke isn't on them, and no, they don't have they wrong person. The joke is on me. Me, Brian Collins, the one that left an apartment in such a disarray. I just happened to be in the wrong place at the wrong time tonight. *Shit!*

The officer asks if I have an attorney I'd like to call. I nod my head, no. Hell, I can barely afford to pay for any food much less keep a damn lawyer on speed dial. I just know that my needing a lawyer means this is more than just something petty. What the hell have I gotten myself into now?

He continues by saying that one will be appointed to me and that I'll be staying in a holding room for the night. Come morning, we'll process your case further.

I cooperate and figure there's no sense in fighting now.

****

The next morning, I eat the measly meal they provide and do everything according to their instructions. If I do what they tell me and the attorney is able to pull some strings, maybe this won't be so bad after all.

About ten-thirty in the morning—according to the clock I'm able to see down the hallway—an officer shows up for me. I'm escorted to some kind of conference-like room. There, seated at the table is my court-appointed attorney. I'd expected to see some short and dumpy, overweight man with a mismatched suit and receding hairline, but the person sitting across from me doesn't fit that description at all. In fact, *she's* nothing like that. That's right, I said she.

She introduces herself as Connie Parker and stands to shake my hand. Ms. Parker is probably five foot seven with long, straight brown hair. She has on a fair amount of make-up that accentuates her rather basic outfit of tan slacks and white button-down collared shirt. I couldn't tell if she was wearing heels or not. Her blouse is stretched tight across her breasts, and I look away the moment she catches me staring at her cleavage.

I wonder if she had any idea that her client was a sexually-deprived twenty-two-year-old? Come on, my wife bailed on me. It's been a while since I've had any.

Ms. Parker appears to be in her late twenties, maybe, but there's no way she could be more than thirty-one or thirty-two. The only jewelry she wears is a silver-banded watch. I wonder if she's single, since she clearly didn't have on a ring, or did she have one of those mornings where she was running late and just walked out of the house forgetting to put them on. And, if the latter is the case, does she feel naked now that I've examined her appearance? I've heard women make that statement before and wondered what it must feel like.

Connie, as she prefers to be called, doesn't waste any time getting down to business. She starts by asking me a series of questions—similar to those that the officers drilled me with earlier. There's no sense in lying about anything so I'm pretty straightforward with her. She carefully jots down her notes then stops to look at me.

"Brian, do you know what you were arrested for?"

"Uhm, no ma'am. No one really gave me a reason." I have an idea but nothing was confirmed.

She flips to the front of her notebook—after carefully scanning her notes—then proceeds to tell me. "You were picked up because there's a warrant for your arrest filed by Cedar Woods Apartment Complex. Is this where you live?"

"I was, but I'm not anymore."

"So you recently moved?"

I nod my head. "Yeah, I...I left."

"And do you have a current residence that you're staying at?"

I look down at the floor before looking at her again. "No."

According to the warrant, the management staff claimed I caused damage to their property—and not just a little bit, either. I don't really have much to say and figure it's not worth trying to dispute everything she reads off the list.

Honestly, I feel they probably made this into something more than they should've, and it's almost embarrassing hearing everything they claim I did.

Ms. Parker listens to my side of the story and genuinely seems concerned about me.

"Well, Brian, if you don't have anything more to add, then this about does it for the day. I'll be back in touch with you soon." She stands and adjusts her top before walking towards the door where a guard has been standing the entire time.

"Wait, there is one more thing," I say to her. I didn't get much sleep once I was finally put into a holding cell. My mind was cluttered with so much. "I've been thinking. And…"

"Yes, Brian?"

"I'm tired of making things hard on me and everyone else."

"Okay, but I'm not following you. Can you explain this further?"

"I was recently served divorce papers. Looking back on everything, I know neither of us was ready for a relationship, much less marriage. Look at me, do I look like someone that deserves a wife? I don't have a damn thing to offer anyone, including myself. I can't keep a job. My parents don't want me in their lives. I'm a complete fuck-up and a failure. Can you see to it that I get another copy of those divorce papers? I don't want to make this a long, drawn-out legal battle with Jennifer. She didn't deserve any of this. I want to sign the papers and let her be free to live her life."

"Mr. Collins, I'll do my best to see about getting those papers for you. I'll be in touch." And with that, the guard escorts her out the door.

I sit back down in the chair and place my elbows on the table. I lean my chin into the palms of my hands and let out a deep sigh. I know in my heart it was the right thing to do. I don't deserve to be a husband or a father.

Part Two

Chapter 13

Jennifer

Two months later.

SO MUCH HAS HAPPENED IN my life lately.

My baby girl, Chloe, has been home with me for three weeks now, and I'm still adjusting to this sleep pattern we're on. For the first few nights, I couldn't leave her side, afraid I might not hear her cry or even worse, that she would stop breathing.

For the first six weeks of her life, she remained hospitalized until she was healthy and stable enough to come home. She was behind on a few things since she decided to enter the world earlier than expected, but she got around-the-clock care from the nurses and hospital staff and pretty much had everyone wrapped around her little tiny baby fingers. Gradually, she began to put on weight until the doctors felt we were in the clear. They assured me a year from now, no one would ever know she'd been born a preemie.

Of course, being a new mother, I absorbed everything they told. I tried to make sure I went exactly by the book so that Chloe would be fine. My mother told me not to worry so much that she was receiving the best of care. So far, everything my mother said has been true. Now that we are home, Chloe has started growing into her newborn clothes and has even moved up to the next size in diapers.

To say that my mother and Beth have been angels is an understatement. There aren't enough kind words to describe what those two mean to me.

Since there was very little I could do in the beginning because my body was still recovering, I mostly hung out at the hospital as much as they would allow. Mom and Beth took turns staying with me just so I wouldn't go crazy. Eventually I put my trust with the hospital staff and lessoned the number of hours I spent standing outside the nursery window admiring my beautiful daughter.

I started coming home more, and when I was up to it, my mom took me shopping and started helping me get everything ready at the house because Chloe would be coming home soon. Before she was born, I really hadn't prepared my bedroom for her at all. Together, mom and Beth rearranged the furniture so that Chloe's bed would be within a few steps of my own. Now that she's home, I can stand beside her bed and watch her for hours and hours at a time and never grow tired of looking at her.

Mom suggested that I get on a routine—when Chloe was sleeping, I needed to also be sleeping. I just hated knowing I might miss something if I did doze off. Eventually, though, I became so exhausted, I could barely hold my head up. Thank goodness my mom was here because there was one night I slept for over nine hours straight. I woke in a panic because I'd missed feeding Chloe and hadn't heard her cry when she needed changing. I looked over and saw mom holding her while they both rocked in the recliner.

"It's eventually going to catch up with you and your body needs its rest too. You are still healing yourself, Jenn. If Chloe cries out, it's just fine. She's only strengthening her lungs." Ahh, mom...what would I do without her?

I keep forgetting she had three of us that she'd tended to, and with Beth's experience with Todd—they definitely knew more than me with it came to motherhood.

Chloe has been the best thing that has ever happened to me. Period. I look back at my life and everything I've been through this past year and, wow, I've experienced so much. There just aren't enough wonderful words to describe how becoming a mother makes you feel. I stare down at her while she sleeps and it's the most perfect site you'll ever lay your eyes upon—babies are so pure and innocent.

Chloe still doesn't have much hair, but the little bit she does have has a dark tint to it. Mine has always had dark undertones; I just hope hers doesn't get any darker. I admit there are some features about her that do resemble Brian, but I try not to think about it. Chloe will go through so many changes with her looks before she develops her own unique appearance.

Brian has no idea what he's missing out on. If he could've only changed... Things may have worked out differently for the two of us, but there's no way I would ever consider going back to him now. Never again.

As part of the divorce, I requested to have my original last name again. Clearly, that was undisputed. My maiden name was also used on Chloe's birth certificate. I intentionally omitted Brian's name and no one seemed to think it was a big deal. I didn't feel he was deserving to have any rights to her. He's definitely not worthy of being a father, given the path he's chosen to live his life. All has been quiet and I'm not sure if that's a good or bad thing. The last time I heard anything about him was the night dad had called to tell me about the damage he'd done to my apartment. It was also the night I unexpectedly went into labor.

I step out of the shower and glance over at the crib. Chloe is still sound asleep. Sometimes I place my finger underneath her nose just to feel her tiny breaths—I'm pretty sure all mothers do this at some time or another.

I'm not sure if the dress I have laid out on the bed is really what I want to wear this evening, but, if I don't like the way it looks when I see myself in the mirror, then I'll change into something else. You see, Todd is graduating pharmacy school in a couple of hours and he's asked me to come along to celebrate this momentous occasion. While I was happy he invited me, I'm extremely nervous to leave Chloe behind. Of course she'll be in excellent hands with my mother, it's the thought of not having her with me that concerns me.

Todd…where do I even begin on that subject.

From the night he first took me to the emergency room, to just this past weekend when he stopped by to see if I needed anything from the store, there's been this incredible connection between us. Our friendship now is stronger than it's ever been. Lately, though, I've started to feel differently about him. Although neither of us have ever crossed the line, one would think from the amount of time he spends here, that there's surely something in the making.

The night Chloe was born, all of the hospital staff assumed Todd was her father just by the way he tended to me and my needs. When the nurses started asking more questions after he left the labor and delivery room, it was obvious they thought we were married. I didn't want to divulge too much personal information, after all, I had been through enough as it was, but I politely let the staff know Todd was just a really important friend to me. Before I was released, one of the nurses let it slip that I needed to hang on to him—he was surely a keeper.

Now, as I sit her putting on my makeup and getting ready for his graduation, I can't hide the nervous jitters I have. I look out the window and see my mom's car pulling in. She's right on time to tend to Chloe. She lets herself in and I quickly pull the dress over my head and step into my shoes. It feels funny wearing heals, but it's not every day that a girl gets to dress up and accompany a handsome man to his graduation.

"Honey, you about ready?" she calls out from the living room.

"Hey, mom. I'm almost done."

My phone signals an incoming text and I reach for it to see who it's from.

Todd: Planning to leave in about ten minutes. If you need more time just let me know.

Me: That's fine. My mom just got here.

Todd: See you soon.

I fasten the button at the back of my neck and run my hands over the front of the dress, smoothing out any visible wrinkles. Even though the material is somewhat clingy, I'm still a little self-conscious about my appearance. My weight is now five pounds less than what it was when I found out I was pregnant. When I'd first discovered I was having a baby, I was incredibly sick and had lost several pounds. It didn't take long, though, before I started adding on the pounds. I gained a total of twenty pounds while carrying Chloe, and I still have a hard time believing she weighed a little less than four pounds when she was born.

I step back and take one final look at myself. Yes, I'm pleased with the way the dress looks. I just hope Todd likes it, too.

I walk over to the crib to check on Chloe one last time. It's no surprise she's still sound asleep. I'd give anything to get her to sleep this long during the night.

"Wow, look at you." My mom exclaims when I join her in the living room. "Don't you look pretty!"

"Thanks, mom." I can't hide the smile that creeps up on my face.

"What time are you leaving?" she asks.

"Todd should be here any minute. He sent a text just as you were coming in."

"Can you give this to him? Your father and I wanted him to have a little something for all the hard work he's endured to reach this special time in his life." My mom passes me an envelope that she pulls from her purse.

"Sure. Thanks, mom. Chloe's taking a long nap for you so enjoy. Her formula's in the 'fridge. I'm not sure what time

I'll be home but promise me you'll call if you need anything." I'm a nervous wreck leaving Chloe behind but I know she's going to be well taken care of.

Todd opens the truck door to get out but I'm already down the steps and walking around to climb in. I feel bad for not letting him come to the door, but with my hands all sweaty and jittery, I didn't want to make a fool of myself in front of my mom. I think back to that awful night long ago when Todd drove me to meet Rebecca. I'd struggled to get in and out because the truck sat so high up off the ground, but since then, I've learned how to climb in effortlessly. Getting out hasn't been the easiest must I've mastered it just fine. It's definitely a man's truck although Todd doesn't tinker with it and pamper it like most guys do.

I shut the door and get comfortable in the seat as I buckle my seatbelt.

"I could've gotten the door for you and helped you get in," he says, a look of hurt clearly on his face.

"It's okay. I'm…I'm just a little anxious I guess. Here, this is from my parents." I pass the envelope over to him, my gaze quickly darting away when I notice how handsome he looks. He's dressed in black slacks and a white button-down shirt. His striped tie makes him look even sexier than normal. That's right, I said sexier. It's no secret that I see him…well, differently now. "You look nice this evening." I feel my cheeks redden as soon as I say it and turn to look out the window.

"Babe, please don't take this the wrong way, but you look freaking hot."

Now, I know my cheeks are red because I can feel the heat coming from them. He just told me that I look good. No, he said I look freaking hot. That's quite a compliment.

Here lately, I've noticed Todd has started complimenting me more, and I've even caught him staring at me, too. If I didn't know any better, I'd say he's got a crush on me. But who am I kidding? I'm sure the expressions on my face say the same thing. It's just that with everything I've been through, neither of us have ever mentioned the probability of there being something more.

"Todd, you know you're making me blush," I admit, even though it's no secret—I do enjoy hearing him say it.

"Thank you again coming with me to my graduation. It really means a lot that you'd give up your evening for me." He reaches over the console and squeezes my hand.

"I wouldn't miss it for the world." I like the way his hand feels holding mine so I don't bother pulling it away. Maybe it's time I relax…just let things happen naturally.

"How's Chloe doing?"

"She was still asleep when my mom got to the house. I know she'll take good care of her, but I miss her so much already."

I hear my phone ring and reach down to pull it from my purse. I hate moving my hand from Todd's, but I figure it's probably my mom letting me know Chloe's awake now. Before swiping my finger across the screen to answer it, I realize the call is from a number I don't recognize. It's been so long since I've had any harassing calls from Brian, it's only natural for me to tense up.

"Hello."

"Ms. Davis?" I hear the person ask with a questioning tone to their voice.

"This is she. Who's calling please?" I feel a sudden uneasiness—as though I'm about to hear bad news—and I try to steady my voice as much as possible.

"Hi. This is Karen Cooper. I'm Ms. Jordan's personal assistant."

I rack my brain quickly trying to place the name. Then it occurs to me Ms. Jordan is the name of the attorney my father hired to handle my divorce.

"Is everything okay?"

"Yes, I've got some good news to share with you."

"Good news?" I ask, still not sure what to make of the phone call.

"I had instructions from Ms. Jordan to let you know that the judge signed off on your divorce papers today. She figured you'd like to know that's it's all behind you now. It's all over."

I go completely silent, unsure what to say. Todd notices my behavior and slows the truck down to pull off the side of the road.

"Everything okay?" he whispers.

I nod my head and big tears spill from my eyes. This time they are not tears of sadness but rather tears full of joy. I'm officially a free woman. I am no longer married to Brian Collins. All ties with him are finally severed.

"Ms. Davis?"

I hear my name through the phone and quickly try to compose myself to finish the conversation.

"I'm sorry ma'am. I just needed a moment," I tell her. "Your call has completely taken me by surprise.

"I understand. Take your time. I'm sure this must be a tremendous relief for you."

"You have no idea. Thank you so much for this wonderful news."

I turn the phone off and relax back into the seat. I'm speechless.

Todd gives me a moment to regain my composure. It's over. I am finally free.

Chapter 14

Todd

I SUDDENLY GET NERVOUS OVERHEARING the conversation Jennifer is having on her phone, so I pull off the side of the road in case we need to turn around and head back home. I can tell by some of the things she's saying that it's not her mother calling her, but someone else.

I don't want to intrude or come across as nosy, but it's kind of hard not to listen in with her sitting right here beside me. Jennifer becomes quiet all of a sudden and I immediately turn to look at her. It appears as though she wants to say something but she can't form the words. I reach over and take her hand again, just to let her know I'm here for her.

When she finally pulls herself together, she thanks the caller and hangs up. I watch as tears spill from her eyes. I'm a little confused, so I give her a moment before asking if it's okay to get back on the road again.

The rest of the drive into town, we're both silent. I'm scared to bring up the phone call since she looks as if a dam of tears could break at any moment. As soon as we get to the school, I lean over and pull her into a hug.

"I'm not sure what that was all about, but I'm here if you need to talk." I lift up the console that separates us and pull out a handful of napkins. Almost immediately, she leans her head on my shoulder and I can't help but notice how good she feels in my arms.

We stay this way for a few moments before she pulls away. I immediately get out of the truck and run abound to her side. She starts to climb down as soon as I open her door.

"Talk to me. What's wrong, honey?" I place my hands on her shoulders and force her to look at me.

"It's over, Todd. It's finally over." She drops her head down, breaking eye contact with me. She then falls into my arms, and the only thing I can do is hold her. When she's ready to talk, my attention will be solely on her.

I run my hand over her hair—it's the only support I know how to give at the moment. After a few moments, Jennifer finally pulls back from my embrace. Her eyes are red and swollen and most of her makeup is already smudged. She's still pretty to me, but I know she went to a lot of trouble to look extra nice tonight.

"Brian finally signed the papers. The divorce is over." She blurts all in one breath.

I'm speechless and don't know what to say.

"Apparently Brian was arrested a few weeks ago, and while he was working with his attorney on the charges against him, he requested a copy of the divorce papers. He signed without even reading them. Can you believe that? The judge didn't even have to intervene."

"Wow, this is the best news, Jenn! I am so happy for you." I reach over and give her another hug. "You had me so confused. At first, I thought you were upset, but now I see you're emotional because you're so happy."

"Of all the days for this to happen—your graduation day," she exclaims. "I definitely think this calls for a celebration." Finally, a smile appears on her face and she looks as though the weight of the world has been lifted from her shoulders.

"Come on, let's go find my parents and give them the news. I know they'll be pleased to hear this." I place her hand in mine and we walk together towards the auditorium.

****

"Joseph Todd Williams."

My name is called and I advance to receive my recognition for fulfilling all of the requirements for my degree. I am officially a Doctor of Pharmacy. As I near the stage, I hear the applause from the audience, and I turn to look out into the crowd. My gaze is immediately drawn to Jennifer—not my mom and not my dad. It makes me happy to finally see a real smile on her face. Today is not just my day anymore. It's ours—we've both earned it.

I follow the other graduates back around until I'm seated again and wait for the remaining diplomas to be handed out. One by one, the names are called but she's the only thing I'm able to focus on.

I lean forward in my seat to get another look at her. I'd be lying if I said my heart didn't melt. This woman has no idea how much I'm consumed with her. I want to show her the right way a woman should be treated. That is, if she'll let me.

I look down at my watch. It feels like everything is moving in slow motion, but I know I'm just eager to meet up with Jennifer and my parents. Mostly Jennifer, but I know I owe so much to my family for all of their support over the last several years. I was pretty fortunate to be able to attend a university with a pharmacy school that was so close to home.

After the final graduate's name is called, the commencement ceremonies come to a close and all of my fellow classmates disperse in different directions eager to reunite with their families and loved ones. I sort through the crowd until I spot her standing just off to the side of my parents. I run up to them and exchange hugs with everyone. I keep my arm draped around her waist and she's doesn't seem to mind.

The moment is surreal.

Slowly, we make our way through the crowd. I offer best wishes to a few fellow classmates and say goodbye to several instructors. I casually slip my hand around hers as we make our way to the parking lot. This somewhat small display of affection may not seem like much, but for me it's a milestone. The girl has overcome so much I'd hate to make her feel uncomfortable, and at some point we'll share her news with my folks.

My dad announces he has reservations at the **Blue Lake Steakhouse** and if we're going to make it on time, we should plan on leaving soon. He couldn't have picked a better place to eat—they have the very best steaks and seafood, not to mention, the view on Blue Lake is spectacular.

Rather than pile into one vehicle, we agree to go separately from my parents. Traffic is pretty chaotic at the moment, but it shouldn't take us too long to get there. I unlock the truck and this time Jennifer lets me assist her in getting inside. Everything about her seems different now. She's more relaxed than ever before. I ease out of the parking lot and she pulls her phone from her purse.

"I just want to call and check on Chloe," she says.

"Are you going to be okay being away from her for a little while longer?" I ask, not wanting to keep her out if she feels like she needs to get back home. I could always let her take my truck, and I could ride with my parents to the restaurant, but it would mean so much to me if she would accompany me. "I had no idea my dad was planning to eat out."

"Don't get me wrong, I'd love to be back home with Chloe, but I'm also enjoying just being out of the house. My mom was right. I needed a break. Besides, this is a special occasion for you, and I'm honored to be a part of your family's celebration."

As we near the lake, I notice the sun's position in the sky. It's been awhile since I've been out this way, but if it's still like I remember, the sun setting over the water will be absolutely gorgeous to watch from the restaurant's windows. As soon as I turn off the main highway, I point out the number of boats coming in. No doubt, it was a gorgeous day for being out on the water.

I follow the winding road around the lake until it comes to an end. I pull into the gravel lot and drive around until I see my parent's car. Lucky for us, there's a spot next to them, and I maneuver my truck in. Their vehicle is empty, though, so I figure they must be already down at the pier. I help Jennifer climb down then place my hand at the small of her back as we walk towards the water.

"Hey, we're over here."

I hear a familiar voice and look up to see my mom. She and dad are a little way ahead watching a couple fishermen hauling in their catch for the day. As soon as we catch up to them, my mom runs up and gives me another hug. It's not like she didn't hug me enough at graduation, but I know she's proud. Heck, I'm proud of me.

The four of us walk together out onto the pier and stop just outside the restaurant to glance at the framed menu that's posted on the wall. There's so many delicious items to choose from. Dad opens the door and we make our way inside to the hostess stand. A young lady greets us and asks if we have a reservation. After checking her book, she escorts us to a table in the rear that looks out over the water—it's the perfect view. I notice how intimate it feels with the room dim and an oil lamp flickering on the table. I pull out the chair closest to the window for Jennifer then help her get seated comfortably before taking the seat next to her.

The hostess hands each of us a menu then steps aside while our waitress fills the water glasses.

"See anything you'd like to try?" I ask her after she's had a few minutes to browse through it.

"There's so much to pick from, and everything sounds divine."

"I know. There are a couple things I'm considering, but I'm like you, it all sounds so good."

I look through the menu a little longer, still uncertain what I'm going to order. The waitress returns with a bottle of wine and pours a sip for my dad to taste. He nods his head, signaling his approval.

"Mmm, that's pretty good," he tells mom.

I'm not much on wine, but I graciously accept my dad's generosity.

The waitress starts with my dad and works her way around the table taking everyone's food order. When she gets to Jennifer, I notice her hesitation.

"Babe, if you need more time, she can come back in a few minutes," I suggest.

"No, it's fine," she says and closes her menu. "I'll have the blackened salmon, please."

I quickly flip through the menu one last time before making my own selection. "And I'll have the stuffed flounder." As the waitress walks away, I lean over and say to her, "Maybe you can give me a taste of yours."

She smiles when I say it then reaches under the table to hold my hand.

Unsure what to say at the moment, I'm relieved when my dad speaks up.

"I guess now is as good of a time as any," he begins. I look over at mom and notice a smile slowly creeping up on her face. "Well, son. As you know, your mother and I have wanted to go on a cruise for quite some time now. Being the sole owner of the pharmacy, it's been somewhat difficult to make any kind of plans, especially for more than a day or two at a time. Now that you're able to be left in charge, I'd like to announce that we're leaving for the Caribbean in three weeks."

"Do what?" I ask, a smirk on my face. "You're joking right?"

"Nope, son. The pharmacy will be yours for that week. Just don't do anything I wouldn't do." He teases even though he knows I'll do everything in my power to take darn good care of the customers. Being business owners, it's been so hard for them to get away and have a real vacation—they deserve it more than anything.

"Well, there's also something else I'd like to bring up while we're on the subject of the business," he says, looking at me first then turning to look at Jennifer. "Your mom and I have been talking, and, well, it's no surprise, your mom would like to start spending more time at home now instead of working."

"Well, dad, that's a simple fix. Why don't you look into hiring another tech?" I suggest.

"Todd, since you're pretty much going to be in charge now, we thought you should have a say in the matter. And yes, hiring an additional tech will offset some of the workload."

"Okay." I add, a bit confused about where the conversation is going. "But I'm not sure what you're asking of me. Me? A say in the matter?"

"Your mother feels we should hire someone we know; someone we feel is deserving of the job. Since this is our family business and it represents us, we don't want to hire just anyone off the street."

"Do you already have someone in mind? Have you set up interviews?"

Dad looks from me to Jennifer, then back to me again. "We think Jennifer would be an excellent candidate for the position."

"But, dad, what makes you think Jennifer is ready to go back to work yet? She...she just had Chloe and..." I ask and immediately feel bad for not letting her have a say about the matter.

"Son," Dad holds his hand up to stop me from saying anything more. "Why don't you give her a chance to say what she thinks. I already know from talking with her about working and going to school full-time that she's determined *and* dedicated. I want someone with her qualities."

Our table grows silent while all eyes turn to look at Jennifer.

"Sir, I'm honored and shocked all at the same time. I…I don't know what to say." Jennifer stumbles over her words. "I've definitely thought about going back to work, but now that I've got Chloe, I don't know what I would do with her. My parents aren't planning on staying in the area much longer, and I wouldn't have anyone to watch her. I'm honored you would even consider me for this position."

My father smiles as though he was already prepared to hear that response. "I understand. I've spoken with your parents about this already, and they both feel it's an excellent opportunity for you. I hope you don't mind that I took the liberty of discussing this behind your back. The good news is they're both willing to stay a little longer—that is, if you're interested in accepting our offer—until other arrangements can be made with Chloe. Of course, Beth would be the one training you. And, when you feel confident with everything, she'd like to keep Chloe for you. You would start out with however many hours you feel you're comfortable with, then we could progress to full-time hours. Beth would fill in on your days off if the workload demands it."

"Dad," I blurt out. "Please stop this nonsense. You're…embarrassing her throwing all this out at once."

The look on Jennifer's face confuses me. It's almost as if she's actually considering his offer.

"Just hear me out before you say anything," he continues. "There are two other techs that you'd be working with so you wouldn't just be thrown out there on your own. You'll learn at your own pace. And, if you end up liking it, a good friend of mine heads up the pharmacy tech certification program at the university downtown. I realize this isn't what you were already going to school for and that we're looking way ahead, but it's something you might consider. The program is accelerated but we'd be willing to work around that, too. As you can see, we like having you around, Jennifer, and we think you and Todd would work well together."

Jennifer just sits there, speechless.

The waitress, thank goodness, interrupts by delivering our meal. Just when I think we've been saved from this nonsense, Jennifer takes a swallow of her water and clears her throat. Surely she'd not about to say anything.

"Rick, I'm flattered that you would consider me for this position. I know from talking with you and Todd how important the pharmacy is, and honestly, I can't give you an answer right now. It's a lot to think about and I'm flattered that you feel the way that you do about me." Jennifer pauses to take another sip of water. She turns to look at Beth. "It means the world to me knowing you'd not only be willing to train me, but that you'd want to keep my baby, too. Can you just give me some time?"

She brings her napkin up to dot the moisture that's gathered in the corner of her eye. I can tell she is obviously overwhelmed and never saw this coming. Even I'm floored by it all.

Dad, noticing that she's a little stunned, reaches across the table and places his hand over hers. "We just feel such at ease with you. Please, give our offer some consideration, and maybe you can let us know something before we get ready to leave for our trip."

"I will and thank you again. You both have already been so generous."

I offer Jennifer a bite of my fish just to change the subject. I've never had flounder that tasted so good.

I must admit it feels very natural being here with her tonight and I'm glad she came along. I notice Jennifer glance down at her watch and though I hate to say anything, I presume she's about ready to head back home. I've kept her away from Chloe long enough.

Mom and Jennifer excuse themselves to go to the ladies' room and dad motions for the waitress to bring our check. I use the time while they're gone to thank him again for everything.

"Well, I think you took us both by surprise tonight," I say.

"Son, I meant everything I said. She's grown on me and your mother, and I've come to think a lot of her. If I didn't know any better, I'd say you're quite fond of her, too."

My mom and Jennifer finally meet us outside and I notice Jennifer laughing at something my mom must've said. My parents walk on ahead while Jennifer and I lag behind them. I want to reach over and take her hand in mine but I can't muster the courage to do so. I'm just afraid that so much has happened tonight, I'd hate for her to think I'm pressuring her. When we reach the end of the pier, I stop and ask her if she'd like to take a stroll along the water's edge.

She surprises me with her response. "Sure, as long as we don't stay too much longer. I'd really like to get back to Chloe before it gets too late."

"Jennifer, I'll stop by and give your mom a hand," mom interrupts, obviously listening in on our conversation. "Although I'm sure you don't have anything to worry about. What kind of trouble could that precious baby cause?"

"Thank you, Beth. I would appreciate that. And thank you both for including me tonight. You've truly got something to be proud of."

I can't help but grin at her kind words. We say goodbye to my parents, and I hold my hand out to her. It's about time I get over this sudden bit of shyness. "Come on. Let's go."

I lead her over to the paved path that winds its way around the edge of the lake. I think about her wearing her heels and hope it's not too much for her feet.

"I'm not sure how far you'd like to go, so when you get ready to head back just let me know."

"It's so pretty out here," she says after we've walked for a couple minutes. We didn't have anything like this back home."

I realize this is the first time she's really mentioned her hometown. It doesn't seem to bother her, though, talking about it, but I let her steer the direction of our conversation.

We stop for a moment for her to remove her heals. She holds onto my arm to keep from losing her balance then hooks the straps around one of her fingers. I knew they'd eventually start to hurt her feet. "If we need to turn around we can," I mention even though I'm not ready to head back yet.

"No, it's okay. I'm just not used to wearing these shoes," she says. "I've worn flip-flops and gone barefooted around the house pretty much all summer."

"Let's walk out here." I suggest, pointing to one of the piers. I worry about her walking on the concrete, but she doesn't seem to mind. Although we've passed quite a few people out walking and some even jogging, I'm happy we're the only two out here on the pier. It's now dark out, but there's a light at the end shining down on the water.

"Have you ever been fishing before?" I ask her when we're almost to the end.

"No, are you kidding me?" She laughs when she says this. "My dad may like to travel and be outdoors, but he knows nothing about fishing."

I can't help but laugh at her comment about her father. He didn't come across as the outdoorsy type to me either. "We'll just have to see about coming back one afternoon. It's too hot to fish during the day right now, but it shouldn't be too bad once the sun starts to set. Maybe we can even catch enough to bring back home so my mom could fix them for supper."

"I like that idea. Sounds like fun," she says then steps away from me and tilts her head back to look up at the sky. "It's so peaceful out here tonight."

"I couldn't agree with you more. It's a gorgeous night, for sure."

"I guess those must be cabins or something?" she asks as she points to the other side of the lake. Off in the distance the faint illumination of light is barely visible from where we are.

"I'm not sure if those are rentals cabins or if people actually live there all the time. Maybe both. Could you imagine how cool it'd be to watch the sun come up and burn off the fog that lingers just above the water's surface. Pretty spectacular sight, I bet."

"I could stay here forever."

I move over closer to her again, and the nervous feeling I had before returns. I'm standing so close to her that I actually feel the warmth coming from her body. I also notice how even and calm her breathing is, unlike my own.

"Thanks again for coming tonight." I lean forward and place my elbows on the pier's railing then turn to look at her.

"With everything you've done for me, I wouldn't have missed tonight for the world. I'm so proud of you."

The next thing I know, I lean over towards her, close my eyes, and allow my lips to find hers. Much to my surprise, she doesn't resist. We spend the next couple of seconds enjoying each other—the feel of our lips delicately caressing one another. I must admit, I get somewhat lost in the moment, and I think she does, too. We pull apart for air, but immediately allow them to reunite again. I place both my hands underneath her jaws and tilt her head just slightly. The moment is magical, and I resist the urge to open my eyes just to stare at her beauty. I start to feel a little excitement down below so I slowly pull my body away from hers—I'd hate for her to feel how turned on I am just from one kiss. Talk about embarrassing.

"You about ready to head back?" I ask, not really wanting to end this moment even though I know it's getting late.

"I suppose." She takes a deep breath then asks, "Do you promise you'll bring me back out here again? I'd love to see what it looks like during the day. It's beautiful out here tonight, but I'd love to just watch the boats."

"You bet'cha. I'd be delighted to." I feel like a kid again, grinning from ear to ear. *She really wants to see me again.*

We get back to the truck and she allows me to open the door for her. Before she climbs up inside though, she turns to face me again. Closing the gap between us, she stands on her tiptoes and presses her lips to mine again. I slip my tongue just barely inside her mouth and trace it along her teeth. As she wraps her arms around me, I detect I slight whimper from her. I've wanted to share a moment like this with her for so long. The sound of her phone ringing catches us both by surprise, especially with it being so late, and she scrambles to pull it out of her purse.

"Hmm. I don't recognize the number," she says and turns her phone so I'm able to see the number, too. Without saying anything, I can feel the change in her disposition already. Just as soon as it's stopped ringing, it starts ringing again.

"Do you think I should answer it?"

I shrug my shoulders, not certain if it's a good idea or not. For all we know it could just be a wrong number. And, given that it's so late at night, I'm sure we're both overreacting.

"It's up to you," I tell her.

"Hello."

I wait for her to say something to the caller but her face remains expressionless.

"Hello," she says into the phone again.

Suddenly, her eyes fill with tears and she immediately shuts the phone off.

"Baby, what's wrong?" I ask, confused by her sudden reaction. "You didn't say anything."

"Damn it," she cries. "It was him. It was Brian."

"But how do you know that? You didn't recognize the number."

"He...he said my name. And I thought this was all over."

She drops her phone down into her purse then covers her face with both hands while she sobs. I'm so angry. Why did that asshole have to go and spoil our night? I do the only thing I know to do—I wrap my arms around her and hold her. It's got to stop. He can't keep doing this to her. If I have to find the son of a bitch myself, I'll personally see to it that he leaves her alone. For good.

Chapter 15

Jennifer

TODD PULLS OUT OF THE parking lot to head home, and I'm saddened that I let one stupid phone call dampen the evening. Everything was going so well until...until I heard his voice. I was so caught off guard the only thing I could do was hang up. I'm sure Todd probably thinks I'm a baby because every time something comes up pertaining to Brian, I always bust out crying. Why? Why can't I get a better grip? Why do I let him continue to get to me?

"I wish there was something I could say to make you feel better," he says, breaking the silence.

"I'll be okay," I manage to say. "Eventually. I guess hearing from my attorney's office earlier...and now the phone call—well, I thought that meant it was over. Like, you know, really over. That I'd never hear from him again. No more phone calls."

"I'm sorry."

"It's not your fault. I just don't understand why he won't go away. Is it going to be like this for the rest of my life?"

"Eventually he'll stop. And if he doesn't, well, I'll make him stop. I can't believe the only thing he's concerned about, though, is you. How many times has he asked about the baby? Even before you had her, back when he called relentlessly, did he ever ask about her?"

Todd reaches for my hand again. There's such a difference between him and Brian. You can't even compare the two. Todd is…well, he's almost too perfect and is every girl's dream. But no, I had to go and pick the loser. I realize I wouldn't have Chloe and I'm certain I'd never have crossed paths with Todd had it not been for Brian, but…it's just not fair. I don't regret my daughter, but the fact that a part of Brian helped to make her, is something I'll never be able to change. It'd be one thing had we realized we couldn't make it together despite trying as hard as we could, but for crying out loud, it was a one-sided relationship. I was doing everything *and* going to school while he did nothing but lie, lie, lie. My daughter deserves more than a deadbeat father.

Todd pulls in the driveway and I notice he doesn't switch the truck off when he gets to the house.

"Well," he says rather quietly. "Are you going to be okay?"

"I think so. I have to be, right?"

I'm sad the night is coming to an end.

"Thanks again for coming tonight."

"You're welcome." I yawn, realizing how tired I really am. "Maybe I'll see you tomorrow?"

"I'd love that. I'll call you." His smile warms my heart. He gets out and comes around to help me out.

I reach over and embrace him. While I'd love to share another kiss with him, I just don't feel it'd be right given the night's events. Todd stands in front of his truck and waits for me to get inside.

****

The next morning, I roll over and notice the clock on the bedside table. It's already after eight. I quickly jump from bed and head over to Chloe's crib where she's still sound asleep. My mom had just given her a bottle and put her down for the night when I got home last night. Of course, she said Chloe had been the perfect angel, and she told me again how happy she was that I had decided to get out for a little while. Then, I told her about the phone calls I'd gotten. While she was relieved to hear my divorce was finally a done deal, her mood quickly shifted to that of anger and sadness when I told her the other one had been from Brian. Just like me, she didn't understand why he just couldn't go away.

I hadn't realized how tired I really was until I crawled into bed. The moment I closed my eyes, I went straight to sleep.

I think back to last night and the job opportunity Mr. Williams presented me with. Is it actually something I should consider? I know I can't depend on my parents for their financial support forever, and this could be my chance to do something different, to get back out in the workforce again instead of staying cooped up in the house all day. But then there's Chloe. I tear up just thinking about it. I think Beth would make a great sitter, and other than my mom, she's the only person I really feel comfortable leaving Chloe with. She's offered a couple times before to sit with her long enough for me to run into town or if there was any shopping I needed to get done, but I'd always declined.

As I stand here looking down at her in her crib, I realize I could do this forever. Just staring at her smooth, porcelain complexion, hearing her soft whimpers, and watching the tiny bubbles she doesn't even realize she's blowing. Almost like she senses me, Chloe begins to stir. I hurry into the kitchen and begin to prepare her bottle. It's only a matter of time until she cries out letting me know she's ready to eat. I flip the switch on the coffeepot and I'm startled to hear my phone ring. I'm definitely not expecting a phone call so early in the morning unless it's mom just checking in on us. I cringe, though, afraid to see who it is. *Please, don't let this be another call from Brian.*

I can't hide the smile that comes across my face when I see Todd's name on the screen.

I immediately pick up. "Good morning."

"Morning to you too. I hope I'm not calling too early."

"No, not at all. I'm just getting Chloe's bottle ready so I can feed her."

"How did she do last night?"

"She did great. My mom said she wasn't a bit of trouble at all."

"See, I told you that you didn't have anything to worry about."

"I know, but it's still hard. I guess it's good for my mom to spend some quality time with her since she and my dad won't be here much longer. Unless, of course, I take your dad up on his offer."

"My mom made some homemade blueberry muffins this morning. I was wondering if you'd like me to bring you a couple."

"Did she really? Ahh, I bet they're delicious. I just put on a pot of coffee, too. I guess if you don't mind the way I look right now, then sure, I'd love to have one."

"I'll be over in a few minutes then."

I dash back to the bathroom and quickly brush my teeth. Then, I run a brush through my hair. Although it still looks halfway decent from last night, there are a couple loose pieces sticking out. This is going to have to work for now. I hear a knock just as I'm fastening my bra. Chloe starts to cry so I scoop her up and head to the door.

"Morning." Todd says, but I'm barely able to hear him over Chloe's wails.

"Hey." I stick her pacifier in and gently rock her against my shoulder. "Come on in."

"Is she okay?" he asks, a concerned look on his face.

"Yeah, she's fine, just hungry. Can you believe she slept all night? I thought I'd have time to warm her bottle before she got up but she beat me to it."

Todd sets a wrapped plate down on the table then reaches for her. "Here, let me help you. You go on and get her bottle ready."

"Are you sure?" I ask, finding it hard to believe that Todd would be willing to do that. Most guys would shy away from a screaming baby.

"Of course I'm sure." He pulls her out of my arms and places her against his chest. "Go. Get her bottle ready. We'll be fine."

While I wait for the milk to warm in the microwave, I pull two mugs down from the cabinet.

"Todd, what would you like in your coffee?" I call out to him in the living room but he doesn't reply. I thought it got quiet rather suddenly. I look up just as he's walking out of my bedroom. Just seeing my baby in his arms does something emotional to me.

"Everything okay?"

"You bet'cha. All better now." Todd says in a baby talk kind of way then tickles Chloe underneath her chin. He turns her around to face me, and sure enough she's as happy as can be. "I changed her diaper."

"Unbelievable. You changed her diaper? I couldn't even get my dad to do that." I can't hide the little laugh that escapes my mouth.

"Well, had it been anything other than just wet, then I probably would've bargained with you. Otherwise, I handled it just fine."

We walk back to the kitchen to check on her bottle. It feels ready now but when I try to take her from him so I can feed her he pulls back.

"Go ahead and eat. I'll take care of feeding her."

"Todd, no. That's my responsibility."

"Jenn, look. It's okay. I can do this."

"Are you sure?" I'm shocked that he willingly wants to do this for me.

"Yes, I'm sure. Besides, you'll be right there beside us." He lets out a chuckle. "And if I do something wrong, you can scold me."

I can't help but notice the sparkle in his eyes this morning. I'm not sure what's going on with us, but I definitely like it. While the thought of a brand new relationship scares the hell out of me, there's nothing wrong with having a good friend.

I do as I'm told and grab my muffin and coffee and join them in the living room. I'm amazed at how well Todd is doing. When Chloe is about halfway done with her bottle, Todd props her up in his lap and begins to burb her.

"Are you sure you've never done this?" I inquire between bites of my food.

"Nope. Never done it before in my life." He's quick to respond, but I notice the little smirk that's formed on his face.

"Ok. Please tell. There's no way you would just automatically know to do this."

"Well, maybe my mom did give me some pointers," he admits.

"I knew it." I can't help but laugh. "I knew there was more than you were letting on. I need to get the recipe from Beth for these muffins. They are so good."

"Speaking of my mom, have you thought anything more about dad's offer?"

I shake my head no. "No, I crashed as soon as my head hit the pillow last night. Todd, I don't know how I feel about going back to work just yet. I think it's a fabulous opportunity and I'd love to work for you and your family, but the thought of leaving Chloe just scares me. Nothing against your mother because I think she would be ideal to watch her, but I just don't know."

"Please, don't feel like you have to make a decision right now. My mom's eager to be at home more and the idea of her keeping Chloe would be ideal. Not to mention, Dad's a little picky about hiring just anyone. I promise they'll understand if you turn down their offer."

"I'm going to think about it some more."

Todd finishes with Chloe's bottle, and bless her heart, she's almost asleep again. Babies are so lucky. The first few months they spend more time sleeping than being awake.

I stand up and take Chloe from his arms, careful not to wake her. After putting her back in the crib, I turn and see Todd standing in the doorway, watching me.

"Come here," he says, his voice barely above a whisper.

I lay my head on his shoulder and breathe in his scent. I feel so secure being in his arms. I wish I had an answer as to why things happen the way that they do. Todd moves his hand up on my back, and I feel it graze my neck. His touch sends an electric charge throughout my body. We eventually pull apart and walk back to the living room together. I try not to act surprised when he takes the spot beside me on the couch.

"Thank you again for feeding Chloe." I turn to look at him, wanting him to know my sincerity. "And make sure to thank your mom for sending over breakfast."

"I told you, I'm here for you. Now that it's behind me, I'd…I'd like to start seeing you more. If that's okay with you."

"Todd, why are you being so good to me? What did I do to deserve all of this?"

"I knew the moment I saw you there was something about you. There was no way I was going to let Brian harm you. It nearly killed me the first night I took you back. I knew you were going to give him another chance. I guess I couldn't blame you. After all, you were married to him." Todd hesitates before continuing. "I thought about you so often. You just don't know how much. I wondered if I would ever hear from you again. When you first texted me to thank me, I was scared you were going to tell me something bad had happened again. I was relieved you were doing okay, but I was also sad. I would've dropped everything right then and there if you'd needed me to come get you again. Then, as the days passed, I slowly started losing hope." He reaches over and places his hand on mine. "I never told you, but the night you left him...well, I was supposed to be out on a date. A friend of mine had set up a blind date of sorts even though I wasn't keen on the idea. You know I've told you how I felt about dating while I was still in school. I'd only agreed to it because my friend was so persistent and said I needed to get out more. He claimed the world was passing me by and I was missing out on life. Something didn't feel right, so, at the last minute, I cancelled. Maybe it was coincidental that you called, but I don't regret staying home that night."

"Todd, I...I don't know what to say." I'm completely taken by surprise.

"I felt so bad leaving you here alone. I can only imagine how you must have felt, everyday being stuck here in this house, not knowing a single sole and having nowhere to go. I just wish I would've visited you more."

"It all worked out though, and honestly, I didn't mind it. Yeah, I was lonely, but it gave me plenty of time to think about the mistakes I'd made. I learned a lot about me during that time. Besides, your obligations were much more important than me."

"That's not true. Still, I could've put forth a little more effort."

"Please, don't feel bad about it."

"It's just…" He looks away. "I'm crazy about you. I've wanted to tell you how I felt, but the timing was never right. And now that your divorce is finally over, well, I just I couldn't hold back any longer."

"Todd, ……" I open my mouth to say something but nothing comes out.

"I'm sorry, Jennifer. I shouldn't have unloaded everything on you at once." He leans up and runs his fingers through his hair. "You probably think I'm some kind of nutcase."

"Todd." I try again. "Listen to me. It's not that at all. I've cherished your friendship from the very moment you came into my life. I've asked myself a hundred times why did I get stuck with Brian and not someone like you. You've had your entire life planned out for you, you've stuck with all your hopes and dreams, and now you're ready to take on the world. You were focused and determined to succeed. But to find out the way you feel about…me. Don't get me wrong, I…I feel something, too, but you need to keep in mind the baggage that I have. It's obvious I suck at relationships. And being a single mother now…"

"It's not your fault things didn't go well with Brian so stop blaming yourself. It's his loss, not yours. You've got a beautiful daughter that's lucky to have you for a mom."

"But..."

"Jenn, you're beautiful—inside and out. You're smart and fun to be around. Just because you've had a failed marriage doesn't mean you can't still be loved. Don't ever think you don't deserve a second chance."

"Can we just take it slow and see where this leads us?" I ask. "The last thing I want to do is jeopardize our friendship."

"Baby, I'm not pushing you at all. I just couldn't hold it in any longer. After spending the evening with you last night, then listening to my dad's proposition about your coming to work at the pharmacy. I knew that if my parents believed in you enough to offer you a job, then something about this had to be right."

I lean over and let him wrap his arms around me. "You've got a great family and you're not so bad yourself.

Chapter 16

Todd

AFTER POURING MY HEART OUT to Jennifer that morning, I felt it was probably best to give her some space. It was a relief to finally get my feelings out in the open. I let a week go by, the only contact being a text message occasionally checking in with her. I immediately started working at the pharmacy full-time, making sure I was comfortable with everything before mom and dad left on their trip. It kept my mind from wondering if I had made a mistake in telling her how I felt.

Today, much to my surprise, I come home from work and find Jennifer sitting in the living room, deep in a conversation with my dad. Seems mom pulled a fast one and invited her and Chloe to dinner.

As soon as our gazes connect, her face lights up with a smile. "Hey you. How's work going for you?"

"Not bad. Not bad at all. I'm still getting used to a few things and the hours are longer than what I was working before, but I love it."

My dad and Jennifer both look at one another, and I'm a bit confused. It's as though they both have a secret and are holding out on telling me something.

"Well, son. How would you feel about having some extra help?"

"Are you saying what I think you're saying?" I look from dad, then over to Jennifer who looks like she wants to say something so incredibly bad.

She nods her head, unable to control her excitement. "Yes, you're looking at your new employee. It's only going to be for a few hours a couple days a week, but if I like it and do okay, then we'll talk about my going full-time."

"Jennifer, that's fantastic news," I tell her. "I'm so glad you accepted my dad's offer."

"Well, I thought about it a lot this past week then talked it over with my parents. They really want me to finish my degree, but this opportunity is too good to pass up. Having them help from time to time is one thing, but to solely rely on them for everything just isn't right. When Chloe gets a little older and I'm more financially stable, maybe then I can see about going back to school. Or, I just might look into the certification program your dad talked about. I know it's not the same as having my degree but it would certainly look good on a resume. Who knows, I might even consider becoming a pharmacist. But right now, with the holidays coming up, I need to start thinking about Chloe's first Christmas. I can't spoil my baby girl with presents if I don't have any money."

"I'm so proud of you." I lean over and give her a hug. "So, tell me, when you do start?"

"Well, boss, if it's okay with you, I'll see you Monday morning."

****

The following week seemed to fly by in a blur. Jennifer came in on Monday and got straight to work alongside the other techs. I noticed her eyes were a little red and puffy but I didn't bother to say anything about it. I knew it had to be hard on her leaving Chloe, even if it was just for a couple hours. By lunchtime she was already entering prescriptions into the computer and seemed to be enjoying herself. She hit it off with the other two techs—which I knew she would—and even asked if she could take lunch with Jenny towards the end of the week. I was glad to see her making some friends, even if they were her co-workers. This change in her routine seemed to be doing her a world of good.

On Friday, just as Jennifer was getting ready to head out, I stopped her in the back room. "I wanted to let you know you've done really well this week. Both Jenny and Becky commented how quickly you've caught on and you seem to be a pro at this. Thank you for giving it a chance. It means a lot to me and my family."

"Surprisingly, it hasn't been all that bad. Monday was a little rough, but I survived."

"I was wondering, if you don't have anything planned for Sunday afternoon, if maybe you'd like to visit the lake again. I'm sure Chloe would love to take a ride in her stroller around the lake."

She hesitates for a moment before giving me an answer.

"Are you serious? You'd want to take me and Chloe out?"

"Of course. Why wouldn't I?"

"I...I don't know what to say. I'd like to and I think she'd have a blast, but I don't have a stroller yet."

I hear someone walking up behind me and turn to see one of the other techs approaching.

"Sorry to interrupt, but there's a customer up front who needs to ask you a question Todd. Have a good weekend Jennifer. I've enjoyed working with you this week," Jenny adds.

I don't want her to leave without knowing for sure about Sunday, but I also know I need to tend to the customer. "I'll call you tonight and we'll talk more about it. Okay?"

"Sounds good. Talk to you then."

****

Now that the time has changed, I don't like how it gets dark so early now. I stopped off at one of the department stores out by the mall when the pharmacy closed so it feels even later than what it really is. As I pull down the drive, I notice the light on in the living room at Jennifer's place. I'm eager to talk to her to confirm our plans for Sunday, and I'm also looking forward to delivering the box I've just purchased. I hope she likes it and hope this will assure her how serious I am about spending time with her *and* Chloe.

I know I told her I'd call, but I'm dying to see her. As soon as I switch my truck off, the porch light comes on and I look up to see her walk outside. She's changed from the clothes she had on earlier today and looks comfortable in her t-shirt and leggings.

"Hey you," she calls out to me.

"Hi yourself. I'm sorry I didn't call first, but I took the chance you wouldn't mind."

"Come on in. I'm glad to see you." She has no idea how those few words make me feel.

"Aww. Look at Chloe." I walk over to see Chloe laying on the floor with an activity device centered over her. I'm pretty sure she doesn't have a clue what all the gadgets and sounds are, but she's kicking and cooing and having the best time.

"My mom got this for her. Isn't it great? She's really not old enough for it but it seems to entertain her. Well, as long as it's playing music. Once it stops, though, she's quick to let you know about it. I've already been able to get the kitchen cleaned and a load of laundry done."

I kneel down beside Chloe and tickle her little feet. "Hey there Chloe."

"You're running a little late getting in tonight aren't you?" Jennifer says and takes a seat on the edge of the couch. I'm surprised to learn she's paid attention to what time I normally get home.

"I hope you don't mind, but I picked up a little something for Chloe this evening. I also wanted to talk to you some more about Sunday. I hope you'll consider my invitation."

"Todd," she starts to say something then stops for a moment. "Don't take this the wrong way. I'd love to spend the evening with you, but like I mentioned earlier, I don't have a stroller yet. Maybe I can see about getting her one for Christmas."

I quickly interrupt. "Maybe you already have one and you just don't know it yet."

"What do you mean?" She looks at me with a confused look on her face.

I stand up and head to the door not waiting for a response from her. I'm back in no time, carrying a rather large box.

The look on Jennifer's face is priceless. She brings her hands up to cover her mouth then says so kindly, "Todd, you shouldn't have."

"But I wanted to. I hope you like it."

"Todd, it's perfect. Thank you." She rips open the box and I help her pull the stroller out. Other than a couple of attachments, the stroller is already fully assembled. I unfold it and she fastens the printed fabric covering in place. I give it a push forward, then backwards.

"Looks pretty good to me. What do you say we try it out?"

"Are you sure? Here in the house?" She asks almost like this is one of the silliest questions I could've asked.

"Sure. Why not?"

Jennifer leans down to pick up Chloe and I make sure the brake is in place before she puts her inside. She looks so tiny, but I know she'll grow into it. Jennifer fastens the safety straps then adjusts Chloe so that she's comfortable. The seat is slightly angled up allowing Chloe to take in the view while I slowly push her through the house. We make a few rounds before stopping in front of the couch again where Jennifer has her camera out, ready to snap a picture. Soon, Chloe realizes I've stopped and she starts to whimper.

"Awww, don't cry Chloe." Jennifer consoles her but it doesn't help. It's obvious she's ready for another stroll through the house again.

As soon as I start pushing, Chloe settles down. "I think she likes it," I admit.

"I think you're right. Looks light you may already be spoiling her."

I spend the next few minutes pushing Chloe around while Jennifer discards the box. I follow her into the kitchen and notice her pulling out the necessary things to make Chloe a bottle. "And here I thought she was enjoying our little walk. You didn't mention she might be hungry, too." I joke with her and all she can do is smile.

"Well, it is almost bedtime."

"Have you eaten yet?" I ask her.

"No, I got so busy cleaning while Chloe was enjoying herself, I sort of forgot. Maybe when I'm done feeding her, I can find us a something in the kitchen. That is, if you don't mind hanging around for a little while."

"I like that idea...a lot."

I follow her to the living room and take a seat next to her on the couch. I notice the bottle of foot cream my grandfather gave her the day she went with us to the flea market sitting on the end table. "Did you ever use any of this stuff," I ask rather jokingly. Much to my surprise, the bottle is half empty.

"That stuff is amazing," she laughs. "It's no wonder your grandfather stocked up on it when he found."

"What do you actually do with it?" I ask, curious about this miracle cream for your feet.

"I just rub a fair amount on my feet right before bedtime, then put socks on. The next morning, you'd be amazed at the results."

"Hmmm. Let me see your foot," I tell her and slide down to the end of the couch.

"But I'm feeding Chloe."

"No excuses. You've had a busy week and you deserve a little relaxation."

"Todd…"

Chapter 17

Jennifer

THE HOLIDAYS HAVE COME AND gone and I've gotten into a pretty good routine with Chloe. It's hard to believe she's almost six months old and growing so fast. It's amazing how time flies but I wouldn't trade a single moment. I often wonder if Brian ever thinks of her and if he does, does he have any regrets? There were still times that my phone would ring, just out of the blue, and when I'd answer no one would say anything. Each time it'd be from a new number but I knew it was him. I guess instead of reloading the minutes, he'd just buy a new phone altogether.

I'm still working four days a week at the pharmacy, and at the first of the year I started taking classes to become a certified pharmacy technician. Thank goodness for financial aid. I attend classes two evenings a week and during the day on Friday. Beth still watches Chloe and often times Todd relieves her on the nights I go to school. Honestly, I think he was looking for a reason to be at the house more when he volunteered, but I'm okay with it. It's comforting knowing he's there.

We spend a good bit of time together away from work. Sometimes I bring Chloe along and other times it's just the two of us. I feel bad for leaving Chloe with Beth so much, but she swears it's not a problem. She and Rick both consider Chloe their grandchild, and I guess in some ways she really is to them since they've known her from birth.

Todd and I are more comfortable with each other as each day passes, and I don't feel as awkward being caught by his family for sharing an intimate moment. They treat me well, and I couldn't ask for anything better.

This morning when I arrive at work, I notice an envelope on the counter that I didn't recall seeing the day before. I make my rounds to each of the computers, getting them booted up and ready for the day. I also make sure there's plenty of labels loaded in the printers. It's the first of the month which means we'll be busier than normal.

"What's this?" I ask Jenny, the other tech, when I walk back up to the front.

"I believe it's for you," she says without looking at me directly.

"For me? Why would you think that?" I laugh and pick up the envelope. Since it's sealed, I hold it up towards the light but it's no use. "It doesn't have my name on it anywhere."

I notice a smirk form on her face and I instantly realize she knows more about this envelope than she's letting on.

"Just open it." She encourages.

I carefully peel back the back flap and slide out a brochure. A business card stating *"Let us help you plan your next trip"* is attached to the front. I'm a little confused as to why a travel agency would send me something like this—I'm not taking a vacation. I unfold the paperwork that's inside taking note of the destination—Las Vegas. Now I know it's not for me.

"Jenny, this isn't mine. It must be for Rick and Beth. Can you pass me the tape? I need to seal it back up since I mistakenly opened it."

Jenny continues entering something into the computer, completely ignoring me.

"Jenny, did you hear me?"

"Look at it again."

I feel bad looking at someone else's paperwork, but I pull it back out once more. Just above the itinerary I see Todd's name and... and mine? What? Why's my name on here?

The expression on Jenny's face says it all. Someone's been doing a little planning behind my back. I look up just as Todd walks behind the counter. I scramble to put the paperwork back inside.

"Are you okay?" he asks, noticing my struggle with the envelope.

"I'm not...I'm not sure."

"What do you mean you're not sure?"

"This." I hold the envelope up in front of me and suddenly tears burst from my eyes.

"I see you discovered my surprise."

"I don't understand."

"Jennifer," Todd takes both of my hands in his. "Will you take a trip with me? Will you go with me to Vegas, baby? Dad's been so pleased with how smoothly everything's been since I came on board full-time, that he wanted to do a little something for me. And that *something* includes you. This trip is courtesy of mom and dad. He's ready to retire completely from the business now that he's gotten a little taste of what it's like to be at home with mom." He pauses for a moment. "And I believe Chloe may have had a little something to do with it, too. She's...uh...sort of got him wrapped around her little finger."

I blush, not sure what to say about the last statement of his.

"Sooo, what do you say? Will you go with me?"

"Todd, I don't know how I feel about being away from Chloe that long."

"She'll be just fine. Between my parents and yours..."

"What? Did you say my parents? Are mom and dad coming for a visit?" I can't hide the excitement just from hearing that my parents are coming back to visit. Never mind the fact this was all planned behind my back.

"Oh, Todd. How could I say no?"

"Yes!" he exclaims.

"So, when are we leaving?" I look down at the paperwork to see if there's a date.

"Tomorrow."

"Tomorrow? Oh my God," I gasp. "You're kidding me, right? Did you say tomorrow?"

"Yep."

"I don't know. It's all so sudden."

Todd looks at me with pleading eyes. "Please. Please say you'll go. If you won't then neither will I. I don't want to go alone."

"That's not fair. You don't really leave me much choice do you?"

"Come on, Jenn." I hear just off to the side of the room. I turn around and Jenny's leaning up against the doorframe. "How can you say no to that face?"

"You two are terrible, you know that?" I joke.

"Is it a yes then?"

"Yesss, I'd be honored to accompany you to Vegas."

Todd pulls me to him for a hug. "Thank you. I promise, you won't regret it. We're going to have a wonderful time."

I stare at him, unsure what to say next. I've just let Todd talk me into taking a trip to Vegas. Vegas, baby. Eeek, I'm going to Vegas!

He reaches down and lifts my chin up with his finger. "Please don't worry about Chloe. She'll be well taken care of."

"I know. It's just hard. I've never been away from her for that long."

"Unless, you're worried about being alone with me," he jokes.

I can't help but laugh. If he only knew how much I thought about spending *that* kind of time with him. It's so obvious how crazy we are about each other.

****

Later that night, I walk around my bedroom pulling out different clothes to pack. I can't believe I'm going to Vegas. I'm excited and nervous all at the same time. I've never been on a plane before, but that's only half the reason I'm so jittery. I'm actually going to be alone with Todd. I suddenly feel a dampness in my panties and I'm embarrassed to admit he's the reason for it. We've had some pretty intense make-out sessions that have left me breathless and yearning for more, but he's left me in charge of setting the pace in our relationship. He's never tried to pressure me for anything more, and I totally respect him for that. Todd is everything a woman could ever ask for but how much longer can we go on before one of us needs more.

I'm caught up in my own little world, running around like crazy. Do I pack this? Will I need that? Chloe's perfectly content watching television while she swings back and forth.

My phone rings and I reach over to see who it is. Todd knew I had a lot to do tonight so I figure it's probably mom or dad checking in with me. I can't hide the grin that appears on my face when I see that it's him.

"Hello."

"Mind if I come over?"

"Um, sure. Is everything okay?" I ask, hoping nothing about our trip has changed. It was hard enough convincing me to go in the first place. I'd hate for something to change last minute. "Everything's fine. I just...I just needed to see you."

Hearing him say those words does something to me. I look down at what I'm wearing and panic—an old t-shirt and pajama shorts. He'll think I'm such a bum. I stop for a moment to think about things. Todd's seen me at my absolute worse so why should what I'm wearing now matter to him? That's one of the things I like about him—he likes me for who I am during the good and bad times regardless of what I'm wearing. He likes me for...me.

A hear a soft knock at the front door. I look over at Chloe before answering it. My precious baby is sound asleep while her swing continues to rock. I answer the door and hope my face doesn't reveal too much enthusiasm from the site of seeing him again. I remember these same emotions when Brian and I first starting seeing each other. Being in love is such a glorious feeling, but I push those thoughts away. I went through pure hell to get where I am today and I will not let memories of Brian take away my happiness.

"Please don't get mad at me," he says in a weird sort of way.

"What do you ......?" He cuts me off before I'm able to finish what I'm saying. Todd presses his lips firmly against mine, refusing to stop kissing me while he walks me backwards to the couch. We pull and grab for each other as though we've been apart for a long time and not just hours. I manage to pull away for air, but only for a brief moment. A rush of excitement courses through my body.

"Are..." *Kiss.* "You..." *Kiss.* "Okay..." *Kiss.* "With this?"

"Mmm hmm." I manage to mumble.

Todd brings his hands to my breasts, and my nipples harden through my thin t-shirt. As his body presses against mine even more, I detect the swollenness of him down below. It turns me on even more.

Wanting him to discover more of my body, I place my own hands over his and glide them over my breasts, gently squeezing them. As if in slow motion, I move my hands down to the bottom of his shirt and allow my fingertips to grace their way underneath. I feel beads of sweat already forming, making it easier for my hands to glide over his skin. Todd pulls away for a moment and lifts his shirt off. Just seeing him shirtless brings on a whole new meaning.

Todd kisses the area just below my neck then works his way up to the sensitive area behind my ear. "Baby, I love you. I have loved you for so long and didn't know how to tell you. Please tell me you feel the same way."

"Todd, I love you, too. I've known in my heart there was more between us than either of us were admitting."

I stare into his eyes, needing him to not only hear my words, but to feel them coming from my heart as well. I notice his eyes are moist and I immediately sit up.

"Todd, are you okay? Did I do something wrong?" Guys aren't supposed to get emotional are they? Is this how I know it's the real thing?

"No. No, you've done nothing wrong, baby. Just hearing you say that you love me, too. You've been through so much, and I know your heart is fragile. I promise I'll be very gentle with it."

This is such an emotional moment for the two of us.

"Are you asking me to make love to you?"

Todd stands and begins to unbutton his jeans. He kicks his shoes off allowing his jeans to slip off easily. I can't stop from looking down at the tight-fitting boxer briefs he has on. Butterflies return to my stomach as I imagine what he must feel like…well, you know, inside me. It's been so long since I've been with a man and now that I've had Chloe, I hope everything still works the same down there.

I allow him to take my t-shirt off and he stares at my firm, round breasts that are now completely exposed to him.

My body craves his touch. Slowly, he begins to massage my breasts and I'm about to go crazy with all of these sensations.

I tilt my head back and arch my chest out for him. As he visits with each one, nipping and gently tugging generously, I let out a slight moan. This pleasurable feeling is nothing less than incredible.

Our mouths meet again for a passionate kiss. Delicately, he fingers the waistband of my panties. I'm thankful I changed into these pink lacy ones when I got home from work. I have to admit I've just started back wearing the pretty ones again. Little did I know I was wearing them — or in this case, removing them — for him.

He gives them a slight tug over my hips and they fall to the floor. He pulls me to him, placing both of his hands on my ass. After a few squeezes, I'm more than ready to discover what's hidden inside those boxers of his. I simply can't hold off any longer.

Instead of giving me the chance to remove his boxers, he slides them down and I find myself catching my breath as I take in the size of him. There's no way he's going to fit inside of me.

Using his knee, he spreads my legs apart. "Are you sure you're ready for this?" He whispers softly in my ear.

I nod my head. "Mmmm. Make love to me. Please."

Todd steps aside for a moment, long enough to find his jeans. "Give me just a second," he says as he fumbles with his wallet to find a condom.

"You sneaky thing. You were planning this all along," I tease.

"I've waited a long time to experience this with you. You have *no* idea," he emphasizes this last part.

We settle back down on the couch together and I spread my legs for him again. I'm nervous, scared, and excited. I try to relax as best I can, knowing that if I tense up in any way, it's only going to make it difficult. I'm already paranoid he's too big to fit.

Before he enters me, Todd slithers his fingers across my mound and stops just outside my opening. "You are so freaking wet, baby."

He carefully inserts two fingers inside me—in and out, in and out. At first he's slow and gentle, but it doesn't take long for him to increase his speed. I clench my muscles around his fingers, willing my orgasm to hold off. I don't want to come this way just yet.

As my breathing intensifies, I motion for him to move closer to me. I'm...I'm ready to feel him inside me. He brushes the head of his penis over my opening, making sure the condom is lubricated enough before he enters me. I can't believe how plentiful my juices are.

Slowly, Todd enters me. "You okay, baby?" he asks.

"I think so."

When he's halfway inside me, he slides back out just a little bit before entering again. He does this motion several times, and I grip the cushions, enjoying the pleasure he's causing. He feels so unbelievably good. Slowly, he pushes deeper until he's all the way inside.

"Relax," he assures me. "If it hurts, I'll pull out."

I let out a sigh of relief when I realize it doesn't hurt at all and begin to move with him. Together, we form out own rhythm and it doesn't take long before I begin to feel my peak.

"Todd, I ..."

"Shhh"

With one more thrust, I let out a soft cry and Todd pushes himself deeper and deeper. The muscles in his butt tighten under my grip. In just seconds, he, too, pants and moans.

Todd drops his head down by my shoulder and I reach up to wrap my arms around him. His body is covered in sweat, and we're both gasping for air. He lifts his head and kisses the tip of my nose.

"Thank you."

"You felt amazing." I tell him, no longer ashamed for him to see me this way.

Todd pulls off the condom, careful not to let anything come out on the floor. He grabs his clothes then turns to face me before going to get cleaned up in the bathroom. "Baby, you are so beautiful."

When it's my turn to get cleaned up, I stop just outside the bathroom. "I almost forgot Chloe was still in the room with us."

"That's one lucky little lady right there," he says while looking over at her.

"She's my world."

"I'm going to make sure both of you are taken care of for the rest of our lives. You're never going to be alone again."

I don't know how to react after hearing him say those words, knowing this man feels the way he does about me and my daughter.

Chapter 18

Jennifer

TODD ENDED UP SPENDING THE night with me that night. Although I think he was a little concerned his parents might say something the next morning once they realized he hadn't come home the night before, he never let on. That became the first night of many that he would sleep over.

We boarded the plane for Vegas late the following evening and because we were both so excited, neither of us were able to nap during the flight. We checked into our hotel room and I couldn't wait to see the view of the city from the twenty-third floor.

We decided to go downstairs to see all of the excitement. As we walked around the casino, the lights and the sounds were so unbelievable. It's just like what you see on television.

Todd insisted I sit down and play a slot machine. I was a little relentless since I'd never played one before, but figured it couldn't hurt to try. I didn't have a clue how to play the thing but continued to mash the buttons until it showed I was out of credits. Slightly bummed, we moved over to another set of machines and Todd inserted a couple of bills into two of them.

In a matter of minutes, his machine hit a bonus round. As we watched the reels spin, I couldn't believe we'd won two hundred dollars so quickly. It might not seem like a lot to some people, but for me, I felt like he'd hit the jackpot.

After we ate, rather than spend all day at the casino, we changed into our swimming clothes and tried out the hotel pool. It'd been so long since I'd seen any sun, I was a little hesitant to remove my cover-up. The pool area was packed with so many tourists, it didn't take me long to realize that none of them cared what I looked like in a bikini. Todd jumped in the water to cool off but I didn't want to mess up my hair. I found a couple of lounge chairs, and before long, I drifted off to sleep.

Later that evening, we attended a stand-up comedy show. It was the funniest thing I'd heard in a long time and it felt so good to laugh. Before going to bed, we ordered a bottle of champagne and some chocolate-dipped strawberries through room service. While we waited for our delivery, we changed into something a little more comfortable. Once the food arrived, we took everything out onto the balcony and shared a toast. The warm, dry air felt amazing so Todd took off his t-shirt and was left wearing only his boxers. Since no one could see us way up here anyway, I decided to remove my clothes, too—all of them. I felt a little exposed sitting out here completely naked but wasn't that what life was all about— taking chances.

We took turns feeding each other strawberries and making a mess with the whipped cream that had been left on the tray. The champagne was a little sweet for my liking, but after my first glass the only thing that mattered was being here with Todd.

Not sure if he did it on purpose, but Todd accidentally dropped one of the strawberries into my lap. Instead of using the napkin to wipe up the chocolate and cream, he kneeled down in front of my chair and began to lick the cream from my leg. My body quickly responded to his touch and I spread open my legs as an invitation for more. Todd reached for the bottle of champagne and gradually tilted it so that a few drops spilled from the top. The cool liquid ran between my breasts all the way down my chest. He sat the bottle down and began to lick the trail, stopping where it pooled in my belly button. His sucking sounds drove me crazy.

We made love that night on the balcony of our hotel room overlooking Las Vegas. We didn't stop there. We also made love again on the bathroom counter and in the plush, comfortable bed before finally calling it a night. I thought the previous night of lovemaking was the most incredible night of my life, but Todd proved that tonight was even better.

On the last day of our trip, we treated ourselves to a massage at the spa. I was also able to get a manicure and pedicure. This pampering was exactly what I needed. There were so many more things we wanted to see and do, but there simply wasn't enough time. We both agreed we would definitely visit Vegas again.

When we got back home, Todd automatically started staying at guesthouse every night, and eventually he moved all his things over. I think his parents are hoping he'll propose to me one day really soon. I'm sort of hoping that he will, too. I have to say, his parents would make the best in-laws. With Valentine's Day only a few months away, you never know. Seriously though, Todd's made it very clear to me as well as both of our families that he's giving me all the time I need to heal. He's willing to wait as long as it takes.

I completed the certification program and officially became a pharmacy technician. Todd's dad eventually gave up working at the pharmacy altogether, and Todd hired a fellow graduate to take the part-time pharmacist position. He didn't mind working weekends occasionally, but made it very clear this was our family time.

The pharmacy continues to grow, and I'm now working forty hours a week. It's more hours than I'd like to work, but I'm finally feeling like my old self again. Not to mention, having the extra money sure makes things easier. It's nowhere near the salary I could be making as a teacher—my original dream to follow in my father's steps—but I'm happy with the direction my life is headed.

Chloe is growing like a weed and is one of the smartest little girls I've ever met. Of course, I owe most of this to Beth. She and Chloe have bonded so well, and I'm thankful every day that Chloe has her in her life.

Chloe has learned a new word— "gan-mamama." I'm pretty sure Beth is responsible for it, but Chloe is, in every sense of the way, her granddaughter. Once Chloe started learning words, I was a little hesitant what I should teach her to call Todd, and right now, she's settled on calling him "Ta-ta." Strange, I know. Todd spends just as much time with Chloe as any real father would their own daughter, but I don't force this on him. It's something he enjoys doing all on his own. And if you didn't know any better, you'd think she was his.

I've not decided what I'm going to do when the time comes once Chloe starts to question her own father. I guess it really depends on where my relationship is with Todd when that moments happens. It's not Chloe's fault Brian is not part of our lives, and if I end up raising her on my own should something happen between Todd and me, then I'll worry about it at that point.

I reflect back on everything I've experienced the past two years, and I never would've imagined I would be where I am today. Chloe turned one back in August and she has forever changed my life. I consider myself pretty lucky to have a wonderful daughter *and* a loving boyfriend.

Christmas ended up being the holiday that Todd officially proposed to me. When all of the gifts had been opened, he pretended to find another one under the tree that had somehow been overlooked. Wouldn't you know, it just so happened to have my name on it. The size and shape of this gift was very unusual, too. It was a tan colored cylinder of some type, approximately three feet long, but wasn't wrapped. I popped the red bow off the end and glanced down inside the tube. I've seen these sort of containers before and figured Todd had probably found a silly poster or something and this was more of a gag-type gift more than anything. What I found inside, though, was not a poster but rather a bunch of white pages rolled up together encircled with a rubber band.

"What the heck is this?" I remember asking.

Todd looked away and I could tell by the expression on his face that this present was something extra special and not the poster I was expecting to see. I removed the rubber band and began to roll out the pages. My breath caught and my hands immediately began to tremble once I realized the papers I was holding were none other than blueprints. Todd had given me blueprints for the guesthouse that showed several additions he wanted to have done, including adding on two bedrooms, a formal dining room, a den and a two-car garage.

I looked over at him, uncertain what to say.

In that moment, our gazes locked, and Todd stood up from his spot on the floor and walked over to me. He pulled a box from his pocket and kneeled down on one knee.

"Jennifer, will you do me the honor of becoming my wife and allowing me to be Chloe's father?" There were tears glistening his eyes, but I knew there was only one answer I could give him.

"Yes." My voice was shaky as I tried to say the one word he was hoping to hear. "Yes, I'll be your wife. Oh Todd, I love you so much." I stood up and we embraced. Chloe crawled over to us and wrapped her little arms around our legs. He scooped her up and placed her between the both of us.

A month and a half later, we were married on Valentine's Day at a little chapel in the mountains. The ceremony was very small and intimate, but it was a magical moment that we shared between my family and his and a few close friends. Rebecca stood by my side at the altar and Todd's grandfather served as his best man. My father walked me down the aisle, and he and my mother officially welcomed Todd into the family. Chloe was able to carry a small basket of rose petals while she held Rebecca's hand as they walked down the aisle. I couldn't be more proud of this new path I planned to take with my new husband.

Once the weather began to warm, construction started on the additions to the house. The two extra bedrooms were completed first since we were eager to have Chloe move into her own room. We decorated Chloe's room in pink and purple, ideal colors for our loving little girl. While picking out furniture for her bedroom, Todd suggested a white bedroom suit with a canopy would be perfect. I, on the other hand, pointed out a set of bunk beds. Todd looked at me, confusion written all across his face.

While standing in the middle of the furniture store, I couldn't keep my secret any longer. I made the announcement I was eight weeks pregnant and we were going to be having a baby. I don't think I'd ever seen him more excited.

In the months that followed, Todd and I grew closer and closer together as a couple and as a family. Looking back, what I thought had been true love with Brian, was just infatuation. What I share with Todd is genuine love.

On November 10th, I gave birth to a healthy 7lb. 6oz. baby girl. Chloe was so excited to finally be a big sister to a real life baby that she could finally hold. We named the new baby Lilly Elizabeth. Although we call her Lilly, Todd's mom couldn't be any prouder that we had chosen to name the baby after her. Beth had done a remarkable job with Chloe, and I'm sure she's going to do the same with Lilly.

When Lilly turned one and Chloe was three, I decided to go back to work at the pharmacy after taking the year off. Beth was able to enjoy a vacation with Rick during this time but she couldn't wait to spend more time with her granddaughters.

One morning, while driving in to town together, Todd announced he wanted to see about adopting Chloe as his own. We contacted an attorney to begin the process and prayed everything would go smoothly. In six months, everything was official and Chloe's last name was changed to match that of the rest of her family. I enrolled Chloe for pre-k in the fall and stared at the pages of her enrollment forms as I printed the name, Chloe Williams. It's been several years now since I've heard anything from Brian and I hope to keep it that way.

Just like any couple, we've had our ups and downs but there's never been any regrets since becoming Mrs. Todd Williams. We are a happy family and nothing could be better.

Todd, Jennifer, Chloe and Lilly Williams.

To Be Continued…

Heart of the Matter

Book three in the Coming Home series

Amy Stephens

Ten years later...

July 1, 2014

To: Jenniferwilliams@yahoo.com

From: BrianCollins@aol.com

Jennifer,

    I realize I'm the last person you ever expected to hear from, and I hope you will at least read what I have to say before you delete this message. I also want you to know I'm not trying to cause any trouble or make you feel threatened in any way. The last thing I want to do is upset you and your family.

    I'd like to start out by saying thank you for reading this far into my message. I honestly didn't know if you'd open the email or just delete it. Second, I know many things have happened in both of our lives over the years, and I want you to know I'm deeply sorry for all the trouble I put you through. There are no words I can say to take away the pain and grief I caused you back then, but I honestly hope you will find it in your heart to forgive me. You are a good woman and I was wrong.

For many years I have wanted to contact you to beg for your forgiveness, but I could never get enough courage to do so. I've even attended some therapy sessions just to try and help me cope with everything. I had hoped, over time, it would get easier to deal with the pain, but it hasn't. Thankfully, my wife has been very understanding and supportive. If it wasn't for her, I'm not sure I would still be here today.

When you left me all those years ago, I made some pretty bad choices. I was hurt and angry and didn't know how to deal with your leaving. You were the only positive thing I had going, and I screwed that up. I couldn't accept that you didn't want to be with me anymore. Rather than causing more turmoil, I should've been doing more to support you and our unborn child instead of being a deadbeat.

I spent a couple of months in jail and realized there was so much more to life. I was a disappointment as well as a disgrace to my family, but I was the only one that could change that. I ended up back home with my parents and thank goodness they were willing to give me one final chance to turn my life around.

At first I had a very hard time finding a job but eventually found one working at a construction site close to the beach. It was difficult working out in the sun all day long, but I managed to stick it out. I made decent money and was able to put a good bit into savings. Yes, you read that right. I started saving up my money and it felt good. I felt proud for once in my life. At the end of summer when the job was completed, my supervisor offered me the opportunity to travel with his company to another site. I was hesitant at first but decided to take him up on his offer. If nothing else, my parents were able to see I was dedicated to the job.

Eventually the work started dwindling down and I made the decision to move back home again. I had a decent amount of money saved up so I enrolled in a couple classes at the university. I had no idea what I wanted to do with myself, but figured after taking some core classes I might find something to interest me. For the most part, I made pretty decent grades and stayed out of trouble. You would be amazed at the person I had become. I also met someone that was patient and willing to help me with a lot of the personal frustrations I was experiencing. You see, after all that time, I still felt bad for the way our relationship had ended and knowing I had fathered a child that I knew nothing about.

I decided to try my hand at teaching and graduated with a degree in education a few years ago. Yes, I am now a P.E. teacher and coach at the middle school I attended when I was younger. Would you believe I love it! I continued to see Grace, the girl I met when I first started taking classes, and we eventually got married. Grace has been such a positive influence for me. She is also a teacher but has taken the year off to stay at home and raise our son, Brady. I was very honest with Grace and told her all about you and the baby. It wasn't easy for her knowing I already had a child, but together, we got through it. The hardest part was trying to talk about a daughter I didn't know anything about. I couldn't tell her one single thing. Not even her name.

My intent for this email was not to brag or boast about my life, but I wanted you to know I've changed. I've grown up finally and made something of myself but it still doesn't excuse my behavior from all those years ago.

A few months ago my father was diagnosed with cancer and hasn't been given long to live. My mom stayed after him to find out why he kept feeling so bad, but by the time he decided to get checked out, the doctors informed him there wasn't much they could do. My mom was heartbroken because my dad had been so stubborn. She stays by his side but he's declining rapidly. We'll be lucky if he makes it another couple weeks.

This leads me to the purpose for this email. Jennifer, you have to believe me when I tell you I'm not the same person you used to know. I worked out all of my problems with my dad and I'm proud to say our relationship now is better than it has ever been. But it's hard knowing he's not going to be around much longer.

My parents enjoy spending time with Brady, but I can't help but feel so guilty because they have a granddaughter they don't even know exists. Hell, I don't know anything about her and it's eating me up inside.

I hired a private investigator, and it didn't take long to find you. After all these years, I had no idea you were only a couple hours away. Please, don't misinterpret my purpose for this message. I've thought long and hard before making the decision to finally send it to you. I know you're going to tell me no without giving it any thought, but I'm going to ask you to search deep within your heart. Is there some way we can arrange for my father to meet his granddaughter? I know her name is Chloe and based on the information from the private investigator, your husband adopted her many years ago. This tells me he is a good man.

Jennifer, I'm begging you to please give this some thought. If there is any way possible, I really want my father to see our daughter before it's too late.

Sincerely,

Brian

Also from Amy Stephens

Cooper: A Holiday Romance

Available now

Chapter One

KATE NORTH SHUT DOWN HER computer for the afternoon and inhaled deeply. She'd waited all day for five o'clock to arrive. Since the upcoming Monday was a holiday, the thought of having three days off from work excited her. Not that she had any specific plans for her extended time off, but knowing she could turn off her alarm and wake when she wanted was reason enough to be in a good mood. Just three days of pure bliss.

At home there was no one to answer to and no one expecting her to wait on them. Just peace and quiet all weekend long. With the weather already cooling off, she planned to sit out on her back porch in the new swing she'd bought for herself and read a good book. If she was lucky, she might even read a couple. The weather called for blue skies and pleasant temperatures. She couldn't ask for anything better. And if it got a little chilly, she'd just grab a blanket.

Moving back to her hometown of Orange Grove last year had been hard, but, so far, she'd not regretted it. In fact, it'd turned out to be a blessing.

Her father's partner at North Insurance Agency had recently retired, and he was beside himself wondering how he was going to make it on his own. With Kate coming back home again, it worked out perfectly. Her father needed help, and the job opportunity was just what she needed.

Since she'd never done that kind of work before, she'd spent the first few weeks getting acquainted with the day-to-day operations. Her father had been in the insurance profession for as long as she could remember, so she was somewhat familiar with the terminology. She caught on quickly and before long, her father suggested she take some classes and get her license as an agent, too. She was a natural with the clients. Being an insurance agent had never crossed her mind until the situation had presented itself. It'd been just what the agency needed. Since coming on board, the business had already shown a substantial increase and stood to get only better.

Like many little girls, growing up she'd wanted to be a teacher, but that had quickly changed after she'd started college. After a couple classes, she realized education might not be her calling after all. She loved kids, but she just didn't know if she'd have the patience to work with them on a daily basis. She was more the assertive and demanding type—characteristics about herself that might not go so well amongst students. It hadn't taken long before she'd swapped majors from elementary education over to pre-law.

It was then that she'd met Lance. They were both in their second semester of their sophomore years, and she'd fallen head over heels in love with him after they'd debated a controversial subject in one of their classes. She was so smitten.

Of course she hadn't won, but he was outspoken, and she liked that about him.

Kate's roommate had invited her to attend a party several weeks later and, low and behold, guess who else was there? None other than Lance himself. They'd paired off and before the night was over, she'd managed to line up a date with him the following weekend. One date led to several more, and before long, she found herself staying over at his off-campus apartment more than her dorm room. They became inseparable for the next two years.

Upon graduation, they'd both been at a crossroads with their future. Lance still had more schooling, but she was at a loss with what she wanted to do as far as starting her career or continuing on with law school. He'd taken her by complete surprise when he'd proposed, and even more so when he'd suggested they make Manhattan their new home. After all, he'd been born and raised there and knew his way around with ease. It also helped that his father was ready to put him to work in the family's law firm.

He suggested she look for a job as a paralegal in one of New York's many fine law firms just to see if it was indeed what she wanted to do. She could always go back to school later on. Kate, though, was an emotional wreck. It was almost too much to process in such a short period of time. She was so unlike her normal self.

Looking back, she should've seen the warning signs. Their relationship had been too perfect. She should've known it was too good to be true.

The wedding was small and had consisted of a few close friends and family members. The honeymoon, on the other hand, was extravagant. Lance had given her a girl's dream honeymoon—a week-long trip overseas to Paris. She had been in heaven.

She'd briefly come back to Orange Grove, long enough to pack all the things she needed for the Big Apple. It was only normal she broke down before leaving out, giving her parents a teary goodbye before starting the new journey in her life. It had been hard enough leaving them when she went away to college, but now she would begin the next phase of her life.

She was uncertain being in a new city, a huge one nonetheless, and not knowing a single person. She'd always made friends easily, but she was thankful she had Lance to help her navigate her way around. He was only a phone call away.

Manhattan was nothing like her small hometown, but she did her best to adjust, all for the sake of her husband. Slowly, she began to like it, especially when he'd treat her to shopping sprees at some of the finest stores she'd ever had the pleasure of visiting. Clothes and shoes were—without a doubt—the way to a woman's heart.

Lance's family seemed to have an endless supply of money, and it hadn't taken long for her to realize that money *could* buy her happiness. His mother always made sure she was pampered in the most luxurious of ways, too, with trips to the spa and salon.

The job search, on the other hand, wasn't as easy as Lance had made it out to be. She was merely an unknown with no connections among some of the most elite candidates. She was a little disappointed Lance's family hadn't done more to help her get her foot in the door. She hated staying at home so much and felt she needed to contribute more to their household. Her husband didn't seem to mind though.

She tossed around the idea of returning to graduate school just to fill the empty void in her life, but she talked herself out of it. The thought of venturing into the city alone still frightened her.

It was only natural she befriended his secretary since she spent more time on the phone with her than she did her actual husband. She knew his hard work would pay off later on, but as it turned out, she got more than what she bargained for.

She'd never forget that cold, winter day.

Apparently, Lance had forgotten all about their lunch date. Although she thought it strange that his secretary wasn't at her desk when she arrived, she'd brushed it off and walked right on into his office. Never again would she barge into a room without knocking first. Ever.

She couldn't believe what she stumbled upon. With his pants down around his ankles, he was steadily pounding his secretary on top of his desk. She had her skirt hiked up around her waist while she belted out fake panting noises with each thrust. Kate stood there staring at them with her mouth hanging open. The worse part of it all was this woman, she'd...she'd considered her a friend. The only friend she'd made thus far. They'd gone shopping together, and she'd had her over to their apartment. She'd never once suspected a thing. She'd attributed his late nights at the office to his excessive workload. Now, she knew differently.

But it didn't end there. When she'd filed for divorce, he had the nerve to actually blame her, saying she just wasn't able to satisfy him in the bedroom. Funny how he seemed to enjoy the previous three years they'd spent together. Up until he'd been caught red-handed!

It wasn't uncommon for them to have sex four to five times a week. She even recalled a time not long ago that Lance demanded it on a daily basis—morning and at night. Even though they were still newlyweds, it wasn't worth bringing up their sex life to her attorney. She just wanted out of the relationship. She wanted it over. Yes, she'd made a terrible mistake in going there, and she couldn't wait to leave. How could a marriage go from being fairy-tale perfect one day to a horrific nightmare the next?

Kate immediately changed, and her heart had turned cold towards all men. Just like the old saying, it'd be a cold day in hell before she ever decided to give her heart away to another man. How dare he blame her for the failed marriage! Once the divorce was finalized, she'd ended up with a nice settlement. He'd needed to save his reputation as well as his family's, and yes, money talked.

Because she'd not wanted to move back in with her parents upon returning to Orange Grove, she temporarily got a one-bedroom furnished apartment. Just before her six-month lease was up for renewal, Kate decided to look into buying a place of her own. She knew coming back here was where she belonged.

She wasn't ready to be an actual homeowner yet, since it was just her, but the new townhomes being built just down from the insurance agency caught her attention. She knew the moment she walked in to tour the model unit, the split-level two-bedroom was perfect for her.

She even worked out a deal with the builder to refer new clients to the agency. It was a win for them both—she'd quote potential buyers a great rate, and he'd complete the sale. She moved into the first completed unit early that spring and watched her little neighborhood slowly develop all around her.

Her settlement money had also come in handy for furnishing her new place.

All the yards were small, but it was ideal for her. Wooden privacy fences surrounded each lot giving her just enough room out back for her swing and several small flower gardens. During the hot summer months, she'd even gotten the courage to sunbathe out back. And since the homes on both sides of hers were still vacant, it hadn't bothered her to be out back lounging in her bikini. She missed her old self, the person she'd been prior to Lance. Her best friend, Dana, had joined her a few times, too.

She was thankful to reconnect with someone who knew her inside and out. Dana was sad to hear that Kate's marriage had turned sour, especially since she was planning one of her own. She'd even held off asking Kate to be her maid of honor until the last minute just because she knew the way Kate felt about the whole marriage thing. It was a sore subject, but she was relieved when she'd accepted.

Kate had even surprised her by planning a bachelorette party. It was only going to be a couple of their girlfriends from high school, but she wanted the night to be special. There were still a few more things to take care of, but in a few weeks, the ladies were going to have one kick-ass party.

Kate locked the office door behind her and walked out to her car. It was still early for a Friday night, but her comfy PJ's were calling her name. She'd done her grocery shopping the first part of the week, so she wasn't going to have to bother with getting dressed the entire weekend. Nope. Her pantry was fully stocked and there was no way she was going to let anyone talk her into leaving the house. She was going to stay cooped up inside, and she dared anyone to disturb her.

About the Author

Amy Stephens is a new adult/contemporary romance author. Originally from Greenville, Alabama, she now lives in Robertsdale, Alabama, just minutes from the beautiful Alabama Gulf Coast beaches, with her husband and son. She is a graduate of Troy University with a Master's in Human Resource Management. She works in retail management full-time during the day and pursues her passion for writing in her down time.

When she's not working or writing, you will find her reading, watching her favorite football team, the Auburn Tigers, her favorite baseball team, the Atlanta Braves, or watching NASCAR. She enjoys spending time with her family and friends.

She is the author of the Falcon Club series: Falling for Him (book one) and Falling for Her (book two). Both books are available now. Don't miss her first series, Coming Home, re-releasing later this year. Don't Turn Back (book one, available November 2015), Never Look Back (book two, coming soon), and Heart of the Matter (book three, coming soon). The Ride Home for Christmas (2014) is her first holiday romance story. A new stand-a-lone holiday novella, Cooper: A Holiday Romance will release November 2015.

For more information, please visit:

www.facebook.com/amystephensauthor

http://www.goodreads.com/amystephens

amystephensauthor@gmail.com

Made in the USA
Charleston, SC
23 February 2016